The Hunter's Daughter

by
M.F. Lorson

Prologue

I could tell right away that something was wrong. When Dad came home from hunting, he didn't scoop Natalie up. She ran toward him, seven-year-old Michelin Man arms reaching for two weeks' worth of hugs. He bent to kiss her head, tussle her hair, pat her back, but he didn't lift her up the way she expected him to, the way he always did, even if she was getting a little big.

His exhaustion was nothing new. Every fall he came back from hunting a little worse for wear. Two weeks in the wilderness with no shower, too much booze, too much man-to-man time, meat-out-of-a-can time. It took a toll on him. It took a toll on all of them. Grandpa Mick and Uncle Andy - they all looked and smelled like bus station transients at the end of a hunting trip. One year Dad came face to face with a bear. Another, Uncle Andy shot a cougar straight between the eyes as it was mid pounce...on him. I'd seen those three in their states of unravel more times than I could count. But something was different this time. It was in the way Grandpa unloaded the trailer at unusually rapid speed, the way Uncle Andy kept asking if he could help with anything, the way neither wanted to stay for dinner or take a shower or anything else they *always* did on the first night back.

Something was wrong, but no one wanted to talk about it. It wasn't till I caught sight of the limp that I realized what was happening. See, Dad had to be careful on his feet. Diabetes snuck up on him at 40, ravaging his body in ten short years the way it did most in 20 to 30. My mother would tell you she had known he was sick all along but that he never listened and was too dumb to go to the doctor. She'd tell you, that is, if she'd bothered to stick around, but she hadn't. The doctors seemed to agree with her. It turns out Dad had probably been a diabetic for the bulk of his adult life. He'd just never gotten a diagnosis, or any of the treatment for that matter.

Years of uncontrolled blood sugar had whittled his nerves down to stumps. The nerves in his stomach couldn't always digest food. The nerves in his fingertips caused him to fumble more often than not, and his dexterity had taken a serious hit in the last six months alone. But it was the nerves that ran down to his feet that really did him in. He had trouble explaining it, but it was as if they were numb. Like If he stepped on a tack he might not even notice. Yet that didn't stop his feet from hurting. Maybe the pain was deep inside, deeper than tissue injuries and bruises, deeper than broken bones. I imagined it like that phantom limb pain that people feel when they've had an arm or leg amputated. What they complain about isn't really there, but who's to say that makes the pain any less real?

That limp meant one thing: We were in for another amputation scare. The first time was due to an infection in his knee, back when I was Natalie's age and Mom was still half a parent. The doctors said they couldn't save his leg. As a contractor, he was always kneeling here, climbing there, scraping his knees and elbows like the rest of us, but diabetes made it so that a simple cut meant a risk of infection, and infection was the real killer. With diabetes, you could lose a leg over the kind of staph infection a healthy person could fight off with one course of antibiotics. The diabetes made it so he couldn't heal. So we prepared for the worst. Dad spent three days in the hospital with his knee hooked up to antibiotics through an IV fluids bag. It was a last ditch effort, one even the doctors didn't seem to believe in. But then, like last minute Hallmark movie magic, the infection went away, and Dad went home with a Band-Aid and strong words of caution from his doctor.

Then there was the Christmas we got stuck in the snow. Everyone thought we should stay at Uncle Andy's house because the roads were slick and dangerous, but you couldn't convince me that Santa would find us there. No way was I waiting another 365 days for the best day of the year. I begged to go home and Dad, being the world's biggest sucker for batting eyelashes and just a hint of waterworks, gave in. All was well and good, right up until the truck slid into the ditch. At eight years old, I wasn't much help pushing. So together, Mom and Dad struggled to get the truck back on the road. It took 30 minutes. Thirty minutes with wet feet in the snow. He thought he'd never get the feeling back in them. When a normal person gets cold hands or feet, they rely on circulation to take blood to all the right places and warm them up. But Dad's circulatory system was a mess. He was sure he'd end up with frostbite and I was sure I was the world's worst daughter. But just like the time before, it all worked out in the eleventh hour. I hoped it would be the same now, but the grimace on his face with each small step made it hard to believe there were any miracles left.

It was three days before he could be talked into going to the doctor, and he only went then because the ceaseless pain made it impossible to work and not working made it impossible to pay bills. The doctors were quick to diagnose him. It turned out he had broken a bone in his foot while out hunting. Thanks to all the nerve damage, he didn't even notice that broken bone and continued to hike and hunt, all while the bones around that bone wore down and began to break alongside it. Dad had been walking on broken bones for a week, but he hadn't felt the difference, not one bit. And then one night, with whiskey in one hand, he pulled his socks and shoes off, only to discover his left foot had doubled in size.

He certainly wasn't the first diabetic to suffer this fate. It had its own fancy name, "Charcot Foot," and like everything else under the sun, diabetics were supposed to look out for it and see the doctor at the first sign of symptoms. If diabetics really looked out for all the things they were supposed to be cautious of, none of them could have jobs, families, or lives. Just about everything bad imaginable was either the result of diabetes or extra dangerous for those who had it. He couldn't have seen Charcot coming and he couldn't have prevented it from happening, but of course his doctors read him the riot act anyway. "This time, Mike," they had said. "This time it's only a matter of time. There are no more preventive measures."

And just like that, Dad went from a full-time contractor to unemployed, rolling around the house on a scooter-like contraption, the kind they gave to kids with broken ankles. It was funny at first, watching him wheel from room to room spinning donuts to make Natalie giggle. At night he would hop off the scooter and chase her around the living room on all fours. Dad was a big man and it made her roar with laughter when he'd sneak up on her, throw his shoulder into it, and mow her over like a rhino on the run.

It stopped being funny when the realization it was permanent really began to sink in. The first few days were okay, but soon the days became weeks and Dad still couldn't put any weight on his left foot. When he was finally able to get a walking cast, he could only be up and moving for short bursts of time. Never long enough to accomplish anything - just long enough to frustrate him. And all the while the nerve pain remained. Before Charcot he had been in excruciating pain, but the tradeoff was that he was still able to walk on his own two feet. Now, he had all the pain and none of the mobility. What was the point in saving a foot he couldn't walk on? We all thought it, but you couldn't tell him that. It didn't matter how many doctors suggested he scheduled the surgery, or how many times we told him he'd be better off. Dad did not want to let go of that foot. I couldn't really blame him. It made me nauseous thinking about him coming out of surgery, a stump where his foot used to be. The thought was terrifying and I was just a spectator. The kind of nightmares he must have had...I didn't allow myself to imagine.

For years Dad had watched in anguish as one symptom at a time he lost control of his body. Now, his foot was coming off and he knew it. The same way he knew sugar could put him in a coma, the way he knew his hands were too shaky for carpentry work, and that like everyone else he loved, Grandpa Mick - his own father - was going to outlive him. The doctors said it was only a matter of time, only a matter of steps, and they were right. He knew it, I knew it. Every day got worse, and soon it was clear that the operation would have to take place whether Dad was ready or not.

When his time was all but out, Dad came up with the plan. A way to use his final steps that would mean something to him. A way to have control at least once before accepting defeat. He gave it a lot of thought and in the end he knew he couldn't and wouldn't live carefully. He could put off the surgery for six months if he was willing to use his foot as sparingly as possible but what was the point? There was no joy in using what was left of his walking ability to travel to and from the bathroom. He had the rest of his life to live carefully. He had one month, maybe two to actually LIVE and he intended to. No, there was no time for careful. Dad would use every last step he had and when they were spent he would call the doctor.

Chapter One: Maura

It didn't take long for Natalie to melt down. In roughly 30 seconds my bright little curly-haired sister was a snot-covered mess. For an eight-year-old, she could give your toddler a run for his money. You'd have thought she was never going to see Dad again the way she carried on. Maybe she was onto something. It hadn't escaped my mind that Dad might not be so inclined to come back. Amputation isn't exactly the homecoming people fantasize about. Whenever I thought about that, I reminded myself that one abandonment was enough. Dad couldn't exactly go on resenting our mother if he followed in her footsteps. He would be back, life would go on, just different than before.

I made a point not to hug him for too long. It was my way of saying, this is no big deal, though we both knew it was. He didn't give me any special talk. There was no perching at the foot of my bed telling me to take care of my sister, or that I was the woman of the house now. We weren't a sitcom family. For the most part, our talk centered around reality television and household chores. He had certainly remembered to tell me when to take out the trash, and there had been a short demo on what to do if the toilet wouldn't flush. That's how a single dad prepares his daughter for 30 days of having absolutely no clue where her father is...where her *sick* father is. No cell phones, no emails, not even an "X" on a map to show where he intended to go. But if the toilet overflowed? By God, I had it covered!

Dad had hitched a flat-bed trailer to the back of the truck. It was the cheapest kind you could get so he built 2-foot wooden walls around it to keep his stuff from falling out the back end. As if the homemade flatbed wasn't embarrassing enough Dad had gone and let Natalie paint the back gate. Her "mural" consisted of the one thing she was obsessed with drawing at the moment. Last year it was moons and stars this year it was eyeballs. My baby sister was no artist. His tail gate which had first been doused in a Pepto Bismol colored base depicted one giant heavily lashed green eye beside a not so equally well lashed winky eye. Symmetry was lost on Natalie. Even if you squinted that second eye was drooping. His "stuff", the stuff that needed all that protecting, consisted of eight red containers of gasoline. three five-gallon jugs of water, a four wheeler, and a tremendous amount of pork and beans. There was more of course, enough to keep you alive in the wilderness for 30 days. But it was the gas and water that made it all so scary, made him look a tad bit too much like a doomsday prepper. I'd never been embarrassed by my father but it made my cheeks hot just thinking of him rolling down Main Street, all decked out in camo with eight cans of gas trailing behind him.

In my lowest moments, I'll confess, I give a shit what people think. Just then I was giving a shit to the tune of, "It's no wonder Mary Anne left him." Which was what I imagined all my mother's old friends would say when they heard he had rolled out of town for 30 days, leaving his two children under the not-so-watchful eye of an elderly neighbor who was known primarily for keeping the local liquor store in business.

I might have liked to have a meltdown of my own, except there was no one around to benefit from it. There was dinner to be made and chores to be done. A sibling to bathe, and to spoil within an inch of her life so she'd relax and for God's sake go to bed on time. Dad had good intentions but even when he was around, I did most of my own parenting and Natalie's too. I knew she would be a mess and I had a plan in place for that. When the sniveling came to a halt I fully intended to swoop in hero-style with a Redbox rental, and popcorn with a bag of M&M's poured on top, a combo that rendered Natalie completely powerless. Praise Jesus for M&M's. They were the ultimate glue for eight-year-old broken hearts. And, well, as far as big sisters go, I was a little bit awesome.

By 8:30, she was in her footie pajamas, fully satiated by the healing powers of candy, Frozen, and a deeply sincere promise that I would watch YouTube tutorials on how to recreate Elsa's braid. In her own words, "This picture day was going to be epic." And those were the last thoughts Natalie had on the night her only remaining parent left her.

Chapter Two: Alex

It was a brilliant move, Mom sending me to live with drunk Grandpa James while she and Husband Number Four took a three-week belated honeymoon in France. They got to get rid of me and ensure that Grandpa felt like a part of the family long enough to leave a sizeable chunk of his assets to our side of the family. Aunt Renata would shit herself when she found out I was staying here - that was the only thing about this situation that had a silver lining. She was an uppity, greedy, old tyrant with plenty of money and not an ounce of affection for anyone save her toy poodle. She'd never sent me so much as a birthday card. Her only nephew and I got zilch...zing...nada! Stressing her out a little felt damn good. Thanks Aunt Renata! Between you and Dad I'm sure I'll turn out completely well adjusted!

Moving from Portland, Oregon - home of glorious food carts, indie concert halls everywhere you turn, and a downtown that could keep you busy whether you had cash on hand or not - to eastern Oregon was not how I had hoped to finish out my 17th summer. I had to admit, though, Grandpa James had made an effort. My bedroom was on the second floor and looked directly over the Umatilla River. If it were July, there might have been some bikini action down there. Late August's river view primarily showcased the hatching of roughly eight billion gnats. But Grandpa James said there were girls in the house next door. Children he was "watching over." Grandpa James hadn't looked past the bottle in his hand in the last 25 years, so I didn't exactly peg him for the caregiver sort. If I had to guess, there was money involved, or liquor, or both. I could fill a book with what I didn't know about Grandpa James. What I did know was that I was supposed to mow the girls' lawn first thing in the morning. Because apparently sending your grandson over to mow someone's lawn is a fully acceptable way to make sure two kids make it through 30 days without parental supervision.

Chapter Three: Maura

The incessant buzzing of the lawn mower combined with its choke, choke, sputter, die, restart, failed restart is how I woke up on the second day without Dad. There is no earthly reason any human should mow their lawn at six am on a Saturday. But there is sure as hell no reason they should mow *our* lawn at six am. The old man next door had another thing coming if he thought this was going to be a regular thing. As far as I was concerned, I'd done a much better job watching over him for the past 15 years than he had me. Like, when his daughter came to visit from out of town it was me who told her what bar he might be found at. Me who pulled his trash out to the curb when he forgot. He was a good man but he was rarely sober enough to tell.

I knew why my father had asked him to watch us: 1. He was the least likely person to call child protective services, and 2. He had done a good thing for us once. In my father's eyes, a one-time good deed got you a lifetime in his good favor.

Mr. James's one-time good deed happens to coincide with the only time I remember him being sober. It was shortly after his wife died. Mr. James's wife had a good deal of money and she'd left it all to him, nothing for the kids. Everything for him, with one stipulation: that he enter a 28-day program. He had done it, not for the money, but because he loved her something fierce and for a while that had been motivation enough.

It was during this time that he played an important role in my life. It was right after my mother left. I was ten, and angry or sad or whatever you want to call it. When a child is hurting, it's a burden they can't hide, and Mr. James and everyone else in town could see it from a mile away. But whereas my mother's friends brought casseroles and unwelcome hugs, Mr. James did something different. Something that actually helped. He just showed up every day after school. Maybe my father asked him to look out for me, maybe he decided to do it on his own. I hadn't ever asked. But he showed up, threw bread in the toaster, tossed me a soda and sat on our couch watching bad Nickelodeon with me until Dad got home. We didn't talk. We didn't play board games or bake cookies. But it quelled the loneliness my mother had left, even if it was just a few hours a day. I tried to keep these things in mind when I interacted with the hollow shell of a man he was now, but it wasn't always easy.

The likelihood that he was up and mowing my lawn because he had yet to go to bed was a strong one. However, I enjoyed my Saturday mornings sans lawnmower alarm clock. With a great deal of trepidation, I slipped on a pair of flats and headed into the backyard. Had I known there was going to be a hot boy there I might have chosen to wear pants as well.

Chapter Four: Alex

There are worse ways my day could have started than to meet the quintessential girl next door dressed like the beginning of roughly every one of my fantasies. I'd like to say that the sight of her - 5 foot 3, gorgeous tan legs peeking out from a thigh-length flannel, and slightly mussed long dark hair - didn't give me pause. I'd like to say I was a smooth big city guy with the kind of opening line that initiates a short and lusty walk to her bedroom. But what I actually did was stand staring just long enough to kill the lawn mower and start an epic awkward silence in which all I did was repeat over and over again in my head, "Do NOT get a boner."

Not that she could tell. She was, after all, looking directly at my face. An action I probably should have mimicked but had a difficult time accomplishing, all things considered. It didn't take me long to place her. Grandpa James and I didn't have a particularly long and loving relationship but I had visited a handful of times and she was the closest kid in the neighborhood. To be truthful, I might not have ever seen her in pants. It was just more socially acceptable back then to free range as a 5-year-old than it was now. It's not as sexy as it sounds. We used to play together in one of those blue plastic pools they sell at Walmart. The dried ring of grass in her backyard hinted that somebody in her household still did.

Now was the time for words. Only I couldn't seem to form any. She took three gingerly steps in my direction, undoubtedly aware that she wasn't wearing pants but too conflicted to turn around and abort mission.

"It's six am...on a Saturday...and you're mowing MY lawn. Which I would assume is meant to be a favor but seeing as how I don't know you..." she trailed off then, at a loss for what else to say. In all seriousness I had a pretty good reason for being there but when you put it that way even I had to second guess myself.

"My grandpa asked me to do it. It's like a chore, a requirement for staying with him."

I'm not sure if this answer sufficed or if she just really wanted to get back inside. But she seemed okay with this.

"Next time you do this chore please do it at an hour when normal teenagers function."

I nodded, clueless as to how to respond, not that it mattered much since she was already making a beeline back toward the porch. "You do know me!" I called after her. "Or you used to." This got her attention. "You taught me how to make Jell-O!" I yelled. The memory flooding back with unexpected vigor.

She turned and smiled. "Oh yeah! I taught you how to make a mess. Lime flavored soup, if I recall correctly." She laughed.

I shrugged. "The details are fuzzy. It was a decade ago, you know."

"You're older than me. You should remember better."

"In my defense," I proclaimed. "I have inhaled a considerable amount of pollution."

"In your defense," she retorted. "I'm super memorable...and classy."

"...and you dress well," I said with a wink. The wink may have been too much. The wink was definitely too much. I felt like an idiot. A shirtless idiot swatting at gnats and trying to conceal a big ass blush from a ridiculously hot girl. I restarted the lawn mower and gave her a wave I hoped looked smooth and without effort. (Looking busy is a very effective method of communicating with the opposite sex.) And then she went inside, where pants probably got put on, much to the disappointment of my overactive imagination.

Chapter Five: Maura

There is a boy next door. A beautiful boy. A boy who remembers me fondly and has NO idea that the majority of the junior class refers to me as Maura Ingalls Wilder, Little House on the Prude. Arguably, a clever insult for a generation of children rather likely to be inbred. I briefly fantasized that that boy next door (whose name I still couldn't remember) might stay just long enough to fall in love with me and short enough to never enter Pendleton High School. After all, school didn't start for another three weeks, a benefit of being raised in a town that lived, breathed, and educated all around a rodeo schedule. Said fantasy was interrupted by the pitter patter of little feet and Natalie demanding milk for cereal, which of course we didn't have. Another thing we didn't have was a car, or a license for that matter, since up until now there had been no reason to get one. Everywhere in Pendleton was within walking distance. Sure, Dad would have been thrilled to teach me how to drive and to pick out some completely irrational vehicle to spend countless hours tooling around with, it hadn't seemed worth it to me to risk operating a piece of machinery that killed more people per year than guns, simply to avoid walking in the rain. Now however, while the gnats were swarming like locusts and multiplying like bunnies, the idea of walking to and from the store with armfuls of groceries was less appealing than ever.

A thought occurred to me, the kind I usually brushed off on account of fear, previous experiences of rejection, and general all-encompassing insecurity. I could ask the boy to drive us. After all, his grandpa was supposed to watch over us, and Mr. James surely couldn't drive, so... it wasn't completely out of line. I threw on a pair of jeans and tugged Natalie out the door before I could talk myself out of it. Besides, I had a child, which in itself was a very convincing excuse. She was small and loveable; you couldn't say no to her and still consider yourself a good person.

Chapter Six: Alex

I had this thought, right before the knock. I should make her lime Jell-O. People bring new neighbors things all the time, right? Cookies and shit? And she had a little sister so there was even a possibility someone would eat it and it would not only be a nice gesture but also, like, sustenance. In Portland, you don't have to make friends this way. I very quickly decided not to make her Jell-O. For two reasons, really: 1. We didn't have any. In fact Grandpa James didn't appear to subsist on any form of food. Which was concerning, but a concern I would deal with on another day, and 2.

Because a quick internet search revealed that gelatin was actually made of horse hooves, which left my vegetarian ass supremely repulsed. Fortunately, I didn't have to come up with an excuse to go to her because there she was, standing hand-in-hand with her butterball of a sister and attempting to knock on the hard part of our permanently-open screen door.

"We need you to take us shopping!" proclaimed the little one. "Now! For cereal. It's kind of a cereal emergency."

"Emergency eh?" I tried hard to appear as if I were taking her seriously. A difficult task when it didn't appear that she had missed many meals.

"It's more of a generic grocery run, really," said her sister. "On account of we don't drive and Dad didn't remember that things like food and beverages are as integral to survival as toilet paper and renewing your newspaper subscription."

"I see," I replied.

"It's not a big deal if you're busy."

"No...no...I am definitely NOT busy. Just let me tell Grandpa I'm taking the truck." The little one reached for the screen door. "Wait!" I hollered, semi-embarrassed by the urgency my voice betrayed. "Wait on the porch, please. It's a mess and Grandpa's not expecting you."

That was an understatement. Grandpa James wasn't ever expecting anyone. I'm not entirely sure he even realized I was there. It had been 48 hours and he still hadn't done much more than grunt in my general direction. It was possible that he would growl something unintelligible from the back room, but mostly I didn't want the girls crossing the threshold because I was afraid they would notice the state we were living in. I'd only been there a day so you really couldn't blame me for the mess, but that didn't make it less embarrassing. To put it gently, the living room appeared to be the scene of one too many frat parties. If you looked closely enough there were actually shards of broken glass shoved into the corners. It wasn't that Grandpa James didn't attempt to sweep up.

It was that he didn't own a proper broom and instead relied on one of those ridiculous Swiffer Sweepers they are always advertising in infomercials. Maybe if he remembered to buy the pads that go with it, it would have been effective. However, his practice of shoving all floor particles toward the corners of the room left a lot to be desired. I had taken the recycling out before bedtime the night before, which you would think meant the room was free of bottles, but that would be an ambitious assumption since Grandpa James did his best drinking after hours. There were at least half a dozen dead soldiers scattered about the coffee table. The ever-present smell of stale beer drippings mixed with what I assumed was week-old trash made the place absolutely unvisitable for potential dates - and I did desperately hope she was a potential date.

I didn't bother actually checking with Grandpa. Instead I swooped the keys off his nightstand and took his garbled snore for a "Go for it, son!" For a man who didn't drive further than the liquor store he had a pretty sweet truck. His 1959 blue Chevy Pickup looked like it belonged in a car show, not parked on the grass in his backyard. That truck had been with Grandpa as long as I could remember. When I was younger and visited he let me drive it, so long as I stayed off the main roads. (Note to all love-seeking grandparents out there: If you let a ten-year-old drive your truck , you really don't have to do anything else to impress them.) .

There were no seatbelts on the passenger side, so Maura (whose name I had finally managed to remember) had to keep her left arm wrapped tight across Natalie (whose name I had just learned) to keep her from bouncing around on the gravel road that wound around our houses and led down to Main.

"Walmart or Safeway?" I asked.

"Or Gross-Me-Outlet!" called Natalie.

"I am not familiar with the 'Gross-me-outlet'."

Maura rolled her eyes. "It's new. She means Grocery Outlet. She thinks she's funny."

"She's a little funny," I replied. "But seriously, where do you want to go?"

Maura pulled a small fold of tens out of her jeans pocket. "Dad left 400 bucks for 30 days. I'm rationing. Let's indulge the kid and go to Grocery Outlet. They have superior prices and the best selection of discontinued delicacies. Plus, you should get to know the place. You'll be frequenting it regularly seeing as they also have the best prices on discontinued beer."

"Just my luck."

Together the three of us scoured the aisles. Natalie had an affinity for all things sweet so the majority of the trip consisted of her begging and Maura scowling. She was good looking even while employing discipline. I picked up the necessities for Grandpa and me as well. The "necessities" being three different flavors of Doritos and a package of frozen veggie patties. In the future, someone else was going to have to be responsible for grocery shopping in our household. Possibly Maura, because her cart was full of the things normal people eat on a regular basis. Eggs, meat, veggies (though not as many as any food pyramid would recommend) and a copious amount of diet soda. We silently judged the contents of one another's carts. It occurred to me as I gazed down at my basket of products - all easily found at a 7/11 - that I probably wasn't doing a great job of making myself look desirable. I would have to woo her another way.

The entire drive home consisted of Natalie rambling on and on about My Little Ponies. Apparently the plot was too complex to be boiled down to one car ride because the spiel continued long after I had parked the car and began to unload the girls' groceries. It was Maura who finally cut in to say that if Natalie kept talking about the show she was going to miss the latest episode. That shut Natalie up in a hurry. She barely bothered to wave in my direction before hustling up the staircase and bounding through the screen door at the top of their deck.

It was just the two of us now. If I were still in Portland, this would be the moment in which I asked the girl out. But then again, if I were still in Portland and she said no, there was a very good chance I wouldn't see her again. Here, everyone saw everyone, every day, multiple times a day. Yeah...I could hold off on that. Rejection sounded a whole lot better the night before I left town, not two days into my stay. With that in mind, I gave my own awkward and hasty goodbye.

Chapter Seven: Maura

Less than 72 hours into mock-single parent living and I was ready to abandon ship. At this point, I would have begged everything holy for school to be in session. At least when school was on, I could shove Natalie on the bus for six hours. Now, I could all but keep from screaming. One more My Little Pony reference, one more candy wrapper on the floor, and I was going to lose it. Technically, she wasn't old enough to stay home alone, but technically I doubt I was old enough to stay home alone for 30 days. Seventeen-year-olds make poor choices. Didn't Dad know that? I patted Natalie on the head and told her she could use my iPad for the next hour if she promised to be good and not answer the door to strangers. She, being eight and not possessing an iPad of her own, did not hesitate to take me up on the offer.

I changed into running clothes and took off down the block. Admittedly, I am not a fast runner. Being 5 foot 3, with slightly more to love, made my sprint more of a jog but I liked it all the same. I hadn't always loved running. In fact, I used to hate it until Dad insisted I join the middle school track team. To his credit, I knocked off enough pounds to stop being embarrassed to change in gym class and I turned out to like it a lot. I was never a sprinter and absolutely mortifyingly bad at the hurdles, but I had good endurance, which meant I usually placed well in the distance events. As I got older, I quit track in favor of cross country. I guess I liked the nature part of it. There was something immensely satisfying about crunching over leaves and splashing through puddles. It felt as close to graceful as I was ever going to get.

Cross country was really my only activity outside the home. It wasn't that I didn't have any talent. I did...sort of...maybe. I was maybe a writer, but too much of a chicken to let anyone other than Dad read my stuff. As a result of my present lack of participation in anything outside of Cross country, my college applications were pitiful in the extracurricular department. Pitiful like blank. If I had been smart I would have looked at an application 3 years ago, but leave it to me to wait until the summer before senior year to even consider the process. Could you blame me, though? Mom wasn't around to help and Dad had barely graduated high school. How was he supposed to know what steps I needed to take to get into college? To be fair, I wasn't all that sure I even wanted to go to college. What was the point of going to college when you didn't know what you wanted to do? Besides, my GPA was on the low side. The low, low, side of low. The kind of low that gave my guidance counselor anxiety and made my Dad say things like, "There is no shame in going to a trade school." I wasn't ashamed of going to a trade school at all. I just didn't know what I would do there either.

Life was beginning to feel like one of those quintessential coming of age movies. Will she/won't she ever grow up, kiss a boy, drive a car, go to college. The more I thought about it the more I wanted to keep running, right past the "Welcome to Pendleton" sign, straight into the desert. I was my father's child, I had survival skills. It was easy to picture myself as a hermit, dwelling in trees and scaring the locals for fun. It was my lungs and legs that wouldn't let me off so easy. Weeks of lackadaisical summer fun had left me sorely out of shape. I circled back toward home, back toward Natalie. But the thought stayed planted in my mind: If Dad could run away, why couldn't I?

Chapter Eight: Mike's Journal

On Day One they skittered around my camp like frightened mice. By Day Two they were stealing bits of my food. Now, on Day Three, they are all but nuzzling me as they warm their bushy squirrel tails by my campfire. If they are still here tomorrow, I will name them Chip and Dale. No sense getting attached too early. The chubby one makes me think of Natalie. How will she hold up with Maura now playing both mom and dad? I shouldn't have left them. But each day there I was less and less to them than the day before. They are tough girls. They have Mr. James. He'll sober up if he has to. For the right reasons. My girls are worth it and if he looks hard enough he will see there is something in it for him.

Chapter Nine: Alex

There was no logical reason to go next door and also nothing better to do. I had interacted with Grandpa as much as any human could. Which is to say we had watched a lot of American Ninja Warrior. It was all we had in common when it came to TV. He didn't do sports, he didn't do comedy, and he watched way more Sesame Street than any grown childless man should. What appealed to him about American Ninja Warrior was beyond me, but I liked watching people fall in big vats of water as much as the next guy. As best I could tell, he was rooting for the former Marine with the bizarre hippie fiancé. I only even knew that because he held his breath every time the guy climbed the double salmon ladder (if that doesn't make sense to you, you don't watch enough bad television).

Last night Grandpa tried his hand at some "guardianing." He made dinner. Steak, to be precise. When I told him I don't eat meat he looked at me like I'd just said I was born with three livers and the brain of a disabled goat.

"What do you eat?" he asked.

"Things that aren't meat," I shrugged.

"It's probably a good thing you aren't staying long." And that was our longest conversation to date. I felt all warm and fuzzy just thinking about it.

My excuse for going next door was contrived at best. I was going to make cookies - did they perchance have any butter? And sugar? And basically everything else it took to bake things? I figured it was an effective strategy because even if Maura wanted to tell me to hit the road, Natalie was definitely going to go for it. Plus, didn't it make me look good to engage with the sibling? Wasn't that a thing? That shit worked on TV. If this was a Disney special, it would end with me scoring a kiss, right? All I had to do was believe, right? Eh, maybe not so much, but it was worth a shot.

I put on my khakis and a blue flannel button-down with the trademark beanie Grandma Jean knitted for my 11th birthday. (Yes, it still fits. I had an abnormally large head for an 11-year-old). Back in Portland, I had had a girlfriend or two and though they claimed my slightly red curls were attractive, I felt like a Jewish ginger every time I caught a glimpse of them. My hat gave me courage. Courage was needed.

I knocked for what felt like an extraordinary length of time. I could hear the TV in the background, which I figured was an indicator that if someone was home they definitely did not want to interact with me. With this in mind, I knocked louder and louder, with little sprinkles of aggression. I had all but given up when a tiny round set of hands pulled back the curtain to peer out at me.

"I can't let anyone in," said Natalie. "I'm home alone!"

I had to laugh. "Um...I'm pretty sure you aren't supposed to tell anyone you're home alone. Or come to the door for that matter."

Natalie shrugged, "It's my first time."

"I see. Where's your sister?"

"I don't know, out. Doing stuff."

It occurred to me that this was an excellent opportunity to find out more about Maura without having to actually talk to her. "Out with friends? Out with her boyfriend?" I asked.

Natalie giggled. "She doesn't have a boyfriend. She thinks boys are gross and so do I."

I was just ready to give my keen perspective on the matter when Maura popped up behind me. She was dressed in jogging shorts and a tank top. Not typical visit-with-your-big-burly-boyfriend wear, so I figured it was safe to assume she'd been on her own.

"Natalie! You're going to make people think I like girls!"

"You do like girls!" howled Natalie.

Maura's already flushed cheeks turned a deeper shade of red. "NOT the way you're making it sound."

Natalie puffed out her cheeks. "TEENAGERS!" And with that she headed back to the couch, where a telltale music loop let me know she was getting her App on.

"Rest easy chickadee, I won't be starting any juicy rumors. Wouldn't want to piss off your boyfriend would I?" Though I thought it was a clever way of introducing the idea, Maura was obviously uninterested in giving away personal information. She disregarded the question completely, leaving me still wondering whether or not she had a boyfriend or was even allowed to date. She could have been the friggin' homecoming queen for all I knew. An awkward silence began to spread between us.

Praise Jesus for Natalie, who never felt bad about interrupting a conversation...or lack of conversation for that matter. Her little head popped up over the back of the couch. "Are you coming in?" Natalie asked. "I'm not home alone anymore so I can have guests over if I want to."

I looked at Maura for reassurance.

"Go for it. I'm sure the two of you will have a grrrrrreat time." she said, sarcasm dripping from each word.

I thought the three of us might hang out together but the moment we were inside Natalie tugged me toward the living room, and Maura disappeared into the kitchen. The afternoon was not turning out the way I had in mind. In fact, it was beginning to feel suspiciously like babysitting. But seeing as how I had nothing else to do, babysitting an eight-year-old instead of a drunk old man was a nice change of pace.

Chapter Ten: Maura

Alex and Natalie were on the couch, the two of them transfixed by a Disney sitcom about a Dog with a Blog. "Modern Day Mr. Ed," is what Dad called it. In front of me, my laptop buzzed away with Facebook Messenger notifications. I was abysmal at keeping in contact with people when school wasn't in session. There were unread messages in my inbox from as far back as June. They would remain unread because, to tell you the truth, my mind wasn't exactly focused on Facebook.

From my vantage point at the kitchen table I could just make out a tumble of auburn curls peeking out from under Alex's cap. Red heads stood out everywhere but he really stood out here. Even in a flannel and jeans it was clear that he wasn't raised in Pendleton, hadn't grown up on or near a horse and might not know what to do if he encountered one. A local could tell all of that within moments and it wasn't just because new people rarely moved here. His particular blue flannel had a logo of a horse embroidered on the right hand pocket. We didn't have brand name clothing in Pendleton. We had Walmart, Maurices, places that sold overpriced cowboy wear. There were a handful of thrift stores, but there were no hidden gems to be found. How could there be? Everything handed down here was purchased here. The only thing worse than new Walmart clothing is hand-me-down Walmart clothing.

The kids in school who considered themselves fashion conscious would drive up to Walla Walla on the weekends. Dad used to take Natalie and me there at the beginning of the school year. But his foot made it so much harder to get around that neither of us had asked to go anymore. Maybe, if Alex kept coming over and I didn't manage to scare him off, we could talk him into a drive before he went home to Portland. Nat would go crazy for new school clothes. I would go crazy to leave town, even just for the afternoon. I hated knowing it, but in a lot of ways I was like my mother: Torn between taking care of Dad and wanting more out of life then Pendleton was ever going to offer. Sometimes I wondered if what I felt for her was as much envy as it was hatred. Usually when thoughts like these came along I could just look at Dad, his foot propped in the air, a snore popping out unexpectedly every now and again, and I knew my place was here. But with him gone, it was harder to remember why here was all I had to look forward to.

I thought about asking Alex to stay for dinner but I didn't know what we would talk about. Besides, the three of us usually ate dinner on TV dinner trays with "Jeopardy" playing in the background. It was a tradition that had seemed normal until you figured in the extra person and suddenly the scene looked a whole lot less homey and more depressing. It turned out I didn't have to do any inviting, because as soon as I'd thought it there was a knock at the door. Mr. James stepped in without a moment's hesitation. I couldn't have been more surprised had he been Santa Claus. It had been some six-odd years since he'd last come through our door. Still, I couldn't help but smile at the sight of him. He was older and thinner than I remembered, and the five o'clock shadow across his once-smooth cheeks made him appear rough. Road hard and put away wet, is how Dad would have described him. But I could still see the tiny glint of kindness in his eyes, the one he tried so hard to drown with alcohol.

He cleared his throat as if to announce his presence before addressing Alex.

"Pizza's not meat son. I'm headed to the GP. If'n you're interested." Alex's eyes flicked quickly from Natalie to me. As if anticipating the dilemma at hand, Mr. James spoke again. "You can bring the girls. Hurry along though. I've got things need to be done at home." Natalie didn't give either of us a chance to answer; she was out the door and in the truck before I had time to think of a reason not to go. Alex shrugged his shoulders, swaying awkwardly with his hands in his pockets. "Everyone likes pizza right?" I couldn't argue with that, and I didn't want to.

Together the four of us rumbled into town. Mr. James pick-up, though lovely, was loud. It had a way of announcing you were coming long before you actually arrived. There was a lot of pizza in town but only one place worth dining out, The Great Pacific. The GP, had been a staple in Pendleton for as long as I could remember. It wasn't your typical pizza joint in that it hosted free music a couple times a week, sold what was rumored to be killer beers, and didn't charge you an arm and a leg for your pie. There were also really handsome cashiers. Like, so handsome that I tended to stop there more often than not just to purchase some piddly chocolate bar and gaze into their super-cool hipster-framed eyes. Tonight's cashiers were not a disappointment. They didn't wear name tags but that didn't matter. My best friend Elizabeth and I had given them names at the beginning of the summer. We called the owner's son Dave and the other guy Little Dave, on account of how he dressed and styled his hair exactly like big Dave.

Mr. James ordered the special, which was a Veggie pizza with fresh tomatoes and goat cheese. I hated goat cheese but I didn't say anything. It was free dinner and he was trying. Anyone could tell he was trying. Little Dave brought a pitcher of beer to the table and three soda cups for Nat, Alex, and me.

I figured waiting for the pizza would be painfully awkward but the thing about GP was that there was always some form of entertainment, something you could pretend to focus on when you had nothing to say. The thing I didn't like so much about it was that everyone in town loved the place. You couldn't go in or out unseen, which meant everyone I had avoided all summer was suddenly chowing down in the booth beside me. I'm not some kind of friendless loner and it wasn't like I didn't appreciate having friends, it was just that between watching Nat and taking care of Dad there hadn't been a whole lot of time to spend with other people. I was invited places early on, but by the end of the summer people had quit extending invitations to the girl that always said maybe and never actually showed up.

This did not, however, stop Elizabeth from stopping by our table. After all, the sight of me, some random boy she'd never met, Natalie, and my elderly neighbor didn't exactly go without explaining. And Elizabeth? Well, she was not a shy girl. Whereas it would have taken me several minutes to get up the courage to take a seat uninvited at someone else's table, it took her mere seconds to scout our location and find a chair to pull up. Elizabeth didn't blend in here either. Her family had moved to Pendleton three years ago when her dad got a job at the Municipal Court House. The first thing you noticed about her was her hair. It was big. Eighties big. So big and so curly that it prompted strangers to ask her where she was "From." She must have had a half dozen smart ass replies for this question. The real answer was much simpler. She didn't know. "I'm just a mutt like everyone else here," is what she had told me when I met her family for the first time.

Her family reminded me of one of those stackable Russian dolls. Each sibling was just a tinier version of the one before. Elizabeth was the oldest so being around her three siblings was like hanging out with three of her. Not a single sibling was more than 18 months older than the one before. It meant they all shared rooms and fought without cease.

If Elizabeth was mad at me for not responding to her numerous texts over the summer, she didn't show it. That was one of the best things about her. She left stuff roll off. No drama where it didn't need to be.

"So..." said Elizabeth, "You appear to have made some friends. Care to share?" I felt a gentle kick from beneath the table.

"Elizabeth, Alex and Mr. James. Mr. James and Alex, this is Elizabeth." Alex gave a short wave, while Mr. James gave a short grunt. It didn't take long before it was fairly easy to see that Alex was smitten. There was no faulting him there. Everyone was smitten. I was smitten, for goodness sakes. Elizabeth looked like a Disney princess, all bubbles and smiles, bright blue eyes that stood out from her olive-toned skin so much that she appeared unreal at first sight. The other thing I liked about Elizabeth was that she was NOT smitten, not with anyone, ever. I strongly suspected that her affections leaned a little on the female side, but I'd never asked. If she wanted to say something she would. She wasn't the kind to evoke mystery just for the sake of it. If she didn't want to tell me then she didn't want to tell me and, realistically, I didn't want to know. Pendleton wasn't the sort of town where that sort of thing went over well. If there were gay kids at our school, they didn't talk about it.

What I thought might be a painfully awkward dinner turned into sort of an amazing night out. Thanks to Elizabeth, I didn't have to worry about carrying the conversation and Natalie was over the moon to be eating dinner out. Even Mr. James had a thing or two to say. If you were to walk down the street and catch a glimpse of our table through the window, you might even think we were family. I pushed the thought aside. Dad and Nat and I may not be the cast of "Growing Pains" but we were a family. Sure there were missing pieces, but we worked. The last thing I needed was to start wanting things that couldn't be.

Alex and Mr. James dropped us back home around eight. For the first time all night I glanced down at my phone. Three missed texts from Lizzie. All written during dinner: "Who the heck are these people?" "Where's your dad?" "Have you been making friends without me ;)" Sometimes I forgot how nice it was to have a friend so easy to maintain. I shot her a quick response. "Sorry so MIA this summer. Tell you all about it soon." And I would, just as soon as I figured out what it all was.

Chapter Eleven: Mike's Journal

On Day Four I built the squirrels a bed. "Bed" was a generous term. It was a pile of brush with sticks for sideboards and a miniature lean-to to protect them from the rain. The rain had begun the night before and refused to let up. I wasn't sturdy enough on my feet to hike slick trails, which meant I was holed up at camp until things dried out. (Hence the squirrel crafts.) Maura would snort buckets of diet soda out her nose if she could see me out here tying twigs together for squirrels. We don't even have a cat. Animals are not something our little family embraces. Only Natalie wants a pet, and don't all kids outgrow that desire? Sometimes I ask myself if I'm a bit of a shitty Dad not getting her a puppy, or a lizard, or even that little snail she was all gaga over.

The terrible thing about having too much time on your hands is the way your mind starts wheeling its way through all the things you have and haven't done right. All the things you meant to finish but never did. For example, Nat wanted to be Hermione for Halloween. I'd meant to order the costume. No Walmart for my girl. Something special, direct order from the Pottermore site where all the mega Harry Potter fans spend their life savings. What if she never gets to be Hermione now? It's the little things like that that make me second guess it all.

Chapter Twelve: Alex

The longer I thought about it, the more it irked me. It didn't seem normal for a guy to leave his kids for a whole month. Maura seemed responsible, independent, all that good stuff. But leaving her in charge of everything just to indulge in a long-ass camping trip didn't seem fair. I hoped to God he wasn't out traipsing into the wilderness searching for his spirit animal or trying to achieve some great vision quest. Those things were for movies, not life. I sincerely hoped that Maura's dad was just irresponsible and not some kind of crackpot. The thing about crazy was, it rubbed off on the family.

There was an easy way to solve the mystery. All I had to do was ask Grandpa James, but I was dreading it. He wasn't the gossipy sort but he lived directly next door to them. He had to know more about them than the rest of the people in this town. He'd introduced me to Maura all those years ago so he had to think mostly good things about them, and there was last night. He hadn't hesitated to bring them along. He even seemed to be having fun. Hell, he'd only had one pitcher of beer. That in itself was a mini miracle. He certainly wasn't holding back for my sake. I'd seen him throw back a 12-pack nearly every night I'd been here. Even when I was a kid he drank in front of me.

It was ten a.m. and I found grandpa with a Coors in one hand and a screwdriver in the other. He was tinkering with what appeared to be a long-since-broken can opener while sprawled on the garage floor. To tell you the truth, I was impressed he could get up and down that well. Most people his age don't take a seat on the cement without a forklift nearby to get them back up.

"Can I help with that?" I asked. I didn't ask because I was handy or had any desire to learn to use tools. I asked because I figured it was as good a way as any to get him talking.

"Nope. Just taking the screws out. Don't need any help doing that."

"Riiight, well if I help we can get it done faster, yeah?"

Grandpa James looked up at me as insolent as I've ever seen him. "Uh huh...and if we finish it twice as fast how the hell am I supposed to spend the rest of the day?"

I didn't have an answer for that. I'd never seen anybody approach work like that before. Something must have shown in my face because he motioned for me to pull up a chair. "I'm old Alex. This is what old people do. We fill up our time by wasting it. You see what I'm doing here? I'm taking the screws out of broken appliances and filing them." He shook a box of screws at me. "You think I'm ever gonna use these? Hell no, it's just something to do."

"That might be the saddest thing I've ever heard."

Grandpa James laughed so hard he had to clutch his side. "You just wait kid. It gets worse when you start shitting yourself. You gonna stick around for that as well, or just the summer?"

I knew he wasn't really asking me, but the question still got me thinking. What if I did stick around? Every time Mom got a new husband it was uncomfortable. Kids aren't supposed to have to get used to strangers in their own home. It wasn't paradise here, but there were some perks. Grandpa James didn't care where I went or what I did with my time. There would be no one breathing down my neck about curfew or complaining because I used all my spending money on collectable shoes I would never take out of the box. I wouldn't have to rush getting to know Maura. I could take my time, move slowly, see what she was like at school...and school. A school where your graduating class was less than a thousand had some serious appeal. How many minutes had I spent with trombone in hand, slaving away at painfully long and repetitive renditions of "Pomp and Circumstance," while senior after senior made their way to the graduation podium? Pendleton High couldn't have been bigger than a thousand students total.

The idea of staying was appealing but it wasn't a given. Grandpa hadn't exactly invited me to stay. The question hung between us even if he wasn't really looking for an answer,

Instead I changed the subject. "What's up with the girls next door?"

Grandpa James looked up from the broken can opener he was harvesting for screws. "Why don't you ask them yourself?"

I fiddled with the truck keys in my pocket. "I don't want to pry."

Grandpa smiled, "Son, what you're doing right now is prying."

I knew he would make this difficult. "Just fill me in okay? I don't know them that well and I don't have the nuts to get to know them that well at the moment either."

Grandpa laughed. "Don't you mean her?"

I could feel the blush rising up and over my collar. "Yeah, I mean her."

"You know, you asked me the same question when you were five."

"I somehow doubt that."

"It's true! You said, 'Grandpa, I want to play with that girl next door but I'm shy of her.'

"I did not say 'shy of her'!"

"You absolutely did! You were strangely proper for a tot."

"Well," I mumbled, "I'm still shy of her."

Grandpa scratched his chin. "I suppose you are. What is it you want to know anyway?"

"How about a general overview. Like...where are the parents? Who is she dating etc?"

"How long have you been here?"

I didn't quite get his angle. "A week-ish."

"Right. And in that week did it appear to you that I spend much time worrying about the dating life of teenage girls?"

"I just meant that you might have seen her come and go with somebody is all."

Grandpa sighed. "If you want to know that sort of stuff, you ask her. It's none of my business and also I don't give a shit."

I got it. No point in pushing. "Alright then, her Dad. What's up with that? No one needs to hunt that bad."

"He isn't out there to hunt."

"So what is he out there doing?"

"To tell you the truth, I don't know. But I don't suspect it's good."

"What do you mean, 'don't suspect it's good' ?"

Grandpa tossed the screwdriver at the tool box and took down the end of his Coors. "Enough questions for today."

"I'd like to know more."

Grandpa sighed. "I'm sure there are a lot of things you'd like to know."

There was no sense in arguing. As far as I was concerned, I'd opened the conversation and that was something. The rest could come later. Besides, I was supposed to be reminding him how affectionate he felt toward me, not pestering him.

I wondered if Mom had any idea what her father was like today or if he had ever been another way. My childhood memories here were sparse but good. If my mother had good memories she didn't care to share them. Visiting Grandpa and Grandma had always been about securing a spot in their will. It blew my mind that he had money. He sure as hell didn't live like it. Grandpa's greatest love was beer and yet he wouldn't even spring for the good stuff. How was it possible that he had raised two women as selfish as my mother and aunt? I didn't remember much about Grandma Jean, but nearly every gift she'd ever given me was handmade, so the spendthrift mentality and entitlement didn't come from her.

Sometimes I wished the money was a lie. That Grandpa James could die tomorrow without a penny to leave to either of them. There were days I wished it would all go down like that. But then I remembered how badly I wanted to go to college, how that money wasn't just a luxury for my mother, but an escape route for me. Whenever I felt guilty for being here, I reminded myself that Grandpa James was my only opportunity to go to school. I hadn't wasted the last twelve years sucking up to teachers and taking AP classes just so I could fix cars like my dad and, with all due respect to my mother, I did not plan to pick mates based on income. And truth be known, what was so bad about wanting Grandpa James to like me enough to add us to his will?

Chapter Thirteen: Mike's Journal

I thought about leaving them once before. When I was younger, more selfish. Back when I hadn't quite learned what it meant to be a father. When they had a mother, being a father hadn't seemed to mean as much. I cooked things. I brought home a paycheck, made them laugh, sang the Rubber Duckie song when they refused to take a bath. I didn't think about being integral to their survival, just there for the highlights. I loved them. That seemed enough.

It took their mother leaving for me to realize they had gotten the short end of the stick. I thought all women were born loving, devoted, Mom material. I guess I never noticed that Mary-Anne wasn't a mother-woman. Or maybe I knew all along but pretended not to. I saw what was easiest to see and it wasn't the truth. I'd been stupid.

If I had paid attention I would have seen the signs. Maura seemed to see them all along. She didn't ask for birthday parties or playdates, she never asked her Mom to volunteer in her classroom or chaperone a field trip. The things I didn't know, Maura always had. She wasn't even shocked when her mother left. It was as if she understood, at age ten, that real moms don't leave, or if they do they take the kids with them. It made me angry just thinking about it. What kind of mother didn't even ask to take her children? What kind of mother sent alimony requests but never a letter or a call to her children?

On the day she left, all I could see were her mistakes. But when I looked within myself I couldn't find the things they needed either. I knew without a doubt that I had screwed those kids before they were ever even born. They were meant to be raised in a two parent household. They were meant to have family dinners and picnics in the park. What place did a barely educated contractor have raising two children on his own? I had wild thoughts then. Adoption, abandonment, calls to relatives I thought could do a better job. I thought about it all and in the end I couldn't bear the thought of them being out there in the world with someone else. I didn't want to exist knowing that they knew I didn't choose them. That I was every bit as awful as their mother. I began to see only one way out. Only one way I wouldn't have to watch myself fail them. And then I cracked.

I remember nothing but the adrenaline. My heart exploding from my chest, the fear that drove me to clutch the gun as tightly to my body as possible, the darkness that surrounded me. Voices that called my name from outside. I recognized no one. Nothing was real to me outside of my unwavering belief that the gun was the answer. That the right thing to do was the most wrong thing imaginable.

We had always been part of a tight neighborhood community. You didn't have a crisis without your neighbors knowing. It was no different when I cracked. To this day I can't say who all stood there waiting for me to come out. I felt like a

Chilean miner down there. I could hear them shouting down to me but I couldn't escape. I couldn't crawl my way to the surface despite the fact that the only thing keeping me down there was my own anxiety.

From my crouched position beneath the foundation, their voices were muffled. I could hear them but it was as if everyone spoke a language I couldn't understand. Like dream-speak. The way your sleeping brain knows someone is talking to you and that you should be able to hear them but for some reason you can't put the pieces together in time to figure out what they are saying. Later the neighbors would tell me that the girls were there. That they witnessed everything, that they called out for me and I said nothing, nothing in response to my own children crying out for their father.

What I do remember is Mr. James. Who wouldn't listen to those around him, those who said I was crazy and he ought to mind his own. He told them all to take a hike as he wedged his 60-year-old body into the crawl space beneath our home. His wife had just died and he missed her. Maybe he thought I was feeling what he felt, or maybe he was so numb to the idea of death that he had forgotten fear. Maybe he wished I'd shoot him and then myself. Whatever he expected when he crawled through the rat droppings beneath my house, he was not taken aback to come face-to-face with the barrel of my gun.

I don't know how long we sat like that, or what he said to make me change my mind. What I know is, we came out together in one piece and that the gun stayed there, a forever reminder that it didn't belong in my hands. He never told the neighbors about the gun. He could have called the Department of Human Services, could have had those girls taken away right then and there but he didn't. In fact, he never so much as mentioned that day again. That day in our family, in our neighborhood, became an unmentionable.

Things changed however, in our household, and between Mr. James and I. From that day forward Mr. James came over every day and sat with Maura and Natalie till I got home from work. I had it in my mind that maybe he was afraid I wouldn't come home and that's why he stayed, but whatever the reason he was there when her mother and I weren't.

It took me some time to get my bearings. I didn't become a Dad overnight but by the time I understood just how wrong I had done the girls; it was too late for a quick fix. I spent the next seven years trying to dig the bad memories out of their minds. But Maura was too old to forget. To me, that day under the house was the last day she was a child.

Chapter Fourteen: Maura

I rubbed the sleep out of my eyes and got started on Natalie's breakfast. Bacon and eggs because the longer the breakfast the longer I could put off the inevitable begging. Someone at school had taught her to play Pokemon and now that Dad was gone, I was the one stuck "dueling." I hated it for a lot of reasons but mostly because I was extremely competitive yet too nice to crush an 8-year-old. Letting her win went against my very nature but not letting her win unleashed a fate worse than SAT prep. No one enjoys a crying 2nd grader.

After breakfast the tell-tale whining began, but three slices of bacon and stellar scrambled eggs had woken me up enough to formulate a plan. One I was actually somewhat proud of having come up with: Elizabeth. God bless Elizabeth and her fourteen thousand siblings. Natalie could play with one of them while the two of us caught up on the important things in life, like attractive boys and how often we wanted to stuff our siblings in large boxes with small air holes. Brilliant, yeah?

The two of us plodded over to Elizabeth's, passing a dejected looking Alex along the way. I felt a little bad for the guy. It wasn't easy to make friends here. Pendleton was just small enough that people already had their friends, and without school as a social lubricant it was pretty unlikely he had met anyone. I thought about inviting him along but that would have destroyed the whole point. How could we gossip about him if he was in the same room? I made a mental note to think of something he could tag along on in the near future. A trip to the river maybe. It was still swimmable. Gross...slimy...shallow...and bug infested. But swimmable.

Elizabeth made quick work of Natalie, ushering her and Kate into the backyard with a bag of popcorn, two sodas, and the firm instruction, "No eating while jumping on the trampoline!" Kate was a few years older than Nat but that didn't stop the two of them from playing well. In a town this small, you took your friends whatever age you could get them. Natalie's face was plastered with a smile as she followed Kate into the backyard.

Elizabeth could always take the lead in a conversation, which was a great attribute if you wanted to be friends with me because not only did I royally suck at small talk, I also couldn't stand awkward silence.

"So, you wouldn't know because you don't answer my texts, but I actually had a killer time at Jesus Camp last week." Jesus Camp was a week-long vacation Bible school that Elizabeth's mother insisted on sending all her girls to each summer. At camp, they canoed to the sweet sound of prayer, played simultaneous ukulele renditions of "Our God is an Awesome God," and rocked out to nightly concerts performed by Christian cover bands. Every year Mrs. Fitz prayed that camp would "Turn her children's eyes toward God," and every year camp dug a deeper wedge into the mother-daughter relationship, at least with Elizabeth. It was NOT the type of place for a girl like her.

"Define killer time."

"You know Nikka?"

"Like, Pendleton Nikka? Too much eyeliner, too short skirt, combat boots Nikka?"

"That's the one! Well, apparently her parents had some kind of midlife crisis and decided to get all "Jesus is Lord" up on her ass, so they sent her to Camp Youth for Christ. And it turns out she's kind of incredible. We basically spent the whole week screwing off while pretending to be prayer partners. Good God! You should have heard her during prayer time. It was so effing funny. She would basically pray for the most offensive thing possible and then wait to be called out for it. Only the counselors never call you out for anything. So there she was saying shit like "Dear Lord, please help me to stop at third base this year." "Dear Lord, let my birth control be more effective than last spring." And the counselors just pat her on the back and say things like, 'Thanks for sharing. You'll be in our prayers.' "

"That's amazing. I can't believe I missed that."

"Oh, Maura, you know you're always welcome at Jesus Camp."

"Yeah. When I say I'm sorry I missed that, I am in no way sorry I missed the actual camp part."

Elizabeth laughed. "Usually I would totally agree with you, but aside from Jesus I completely loved it this year."

"Are you two gonna hang out now? Like, at school?"

"Maura Ingalls Wilder, are you jealous?"

"Do not call me that!" I hollered, slugging her with an overstuffed couch cushion.

"Text me back and you won't have to be jealous, ya big whore!" said Elizabeth, smacking me back with vigor.

"K. But in all seriousness, do you think you'll still be friends now that you're back in town? I mean, you weren't before and we've gone to school together since pre-K."

Elizabeth chewed on her bottom lip. "I thought about that. I think so? I mean, we exchanged phone numbers and stuff. We've been texting. It's not like I'm some kind of social pariah. Hanging out with me wouldn't negatively impact her cool factor or anything like that."

I know Lizzie was trying to sound confident, but a part of me was sure that she knew as well as I did that there were definitely things in play that might make Nikka reluctant to spend too much public time with Elizabeth. Like the fact that Lizzie didn't need to say she was into girls for most people at school to already buzz about it. In middle school, someone started a stupid rumor that she and I were lesbian lovers. It meant weeks of torture for both of us. Things only got better when I got my first boyfriend in eighth grade. After that, the rumors weren't that I was a lesbian, just that I was a big fat prude. Which, to be honest, was actually kind of the truth. I didn't know Nikka well enough to know if she could take that kind of social beating in stride.

"Naw," I said. "It will be fine at school. You're awesome, it's indisputable. Jesus Camp is probably the best thing that ever happened to Nikka friendship-wise. I wouldn't worry about it."

Elizabeth wrapped her arms around me in a big hug. "Thanks, Mo." But when she pulled back her face had gone from relieved to concerned. "What about the guy though?"

"What guy?"

Elizabeth rolled her eyes. "You KNOW what guy. The one from the pizza shop, aka the only boy I've seen you with basically ever?"

"Just friends."

"Yeah? He's cute, if you like that sort of thing."

"Just friends."

"You know you could tell me if it was more, right? You know I wouldn't be mad or anything stupid."

I shifted uncomfortably in my seat. "I know."

"It's not like you're having a boyfriend would be some kind of problem. You should date, Maura. If you're into him."

I don't know why I couldn't tell her the truth. The truth was that every time I closed my eyes lately, I imagined him standing in the backyard with that lawnmower. But I didn't say it. For whatever reason, I was afraid to tell her about that sort of stuff. I did my best to shrug and sound natural when I told her, "I'm just not that into him." Maybe I imagined it but it seemed like the tension drained from her face. Not for long, however.

An ear-shattering scream shot through the air. In less than 5 seconds, Kate was flying through the sliding glass doors. "Nat got hurt!"

My heart leapt in my chest.

"BAD!" yelled Kate. "Real bad!".

The three of us burst into the backyard, where we found Natalie clutching her arm on the far side of the swing set, tears streaming down her face. Even from a distance, I could tell that this was no average bump and bruise. I knelt down on the dying summer grass beside her. "What on earth happened?"

Nat was too overcome with tears to do anything aside from sniffling and choking out miserable crying sounds. Kate filled us in, looking at her toes the whole time. "We were seeing who could jump the furthest off the swing. I think she waited to jump till she was too high. She landed on her wrist, I think."

Elizabeth shot Kate a dirty look. "You know you're not allowed to do that! This isn't the school playground. We don't have bark dust to break your fall."

Kate's eyes filled with tears. "It was an accident, I swear."

"Honest!" whimpered Natalie.

"Shit." I mumbled, and then louder, "Shit shit shit shit shit!" Natalie's eyes widened with shock and I was preparing to apologize, preparing some kind of comforting statement when I felt Elizabeth tap my shoulder.

"She needs to see a doctor."

"You KNOW we can't do that."

"Why on earth not?

"Are you kidding me? If I take Natalie to the emergency room, it's gonna raise red flags all over the place. They're gonna demand to talk to my parents and when they can't, they're gonna call child services."

"You don't know that for sure."

"I'm not risking it!" Natalie whimpered in my arms.

"Then what are you gonna do?" she asked.

With Nat still in my arms, I lifted her up to a carrying position. Without the use of her right arm, I had to carry her like a baby - a giant baby. I was gonna start upping her vegetables and lowering her pop tart intake. Good God, she was getting heavy.

"I'm taking her to my summer guardian."

"You have got to be kidding me." said Elizabeth.

"What other option do I have? That's who Dad left in charge."

"What does he know about little kids?"

"I don't know..." I shrugged. "He had them once?"

Elizabeth spoke under her breath, "Yeah, about a gazillion bottles ago."

Nat looked up at me, eyes widening with fear.

"You are NOT helping," I said.

"Sorry," said Elizabeth earnestly. "I just think we need to do more."

"*I* need to do more. *You* just need to keep your mouth shut."

"Maura...."

"I'll call you, okay?"

Elizabeth looked uncomfortable. "Maura, if I don't hear from you, I have to te.."

I glared at her with as much conviction as I had in me. "You WILL hear from me."

Carrying Natalie half, a mile with only one arm to hang on by was no easy feat. I worried about nosy neighbors, but if anyone noticed something was wrong they didn't care to inquire. Not a single passerby asked if they could help. On an ordinary day, a Dad day, I would admonish the town for being so self-involved, but today was different. Today I prayed with all my might that no one would see me coming up the walk with a crying, much-too-old-to-carry child in my arms.

Chapter Fifteen: Alex

On an ordinary day, seeing Maura on my doorstep would have been cause for celebration, but not today. Something was wrong with Natalie. She clung to Maura like a baby sloth, tears streaming down her plump cheeks. I quickly opened the screen door and motioned for Maura to set her down on the couch. There was no time to be mortified by the condition the living room was in, though I could feel a blush rising. I wanted to say, "I clean up every night, I swear!" but I was pretty sure her mind was elsewhere.

Grandpa James came out from the back room. "What's all the com...com...commotion!" There was only a slight slur to his speech this afternoon. They had come at a good time. He was only four beers into his afternoon routine. I looked to Maura to answer.

"Natalie fell off the swing set and her wrist is twice its normal size."

"Why on earth aren't you at the hospital?" Grandpa hollered.

"We can't," hissed Maura. "I don't know who Natalie's doctor is, and even if I did...what do you think they'd say when I can't produce insurance OR a parent?"

Grandpa nodded, then took a knee beside Natalie. "Let me see that wrist sweetheart." With much trepidation, she lay her hand in Grandpa James's. For a moment or two he examined her swollen limb then, scratching his chin, proclaimed, "Maybe we can handle this the old fashioned way. Son, grab me a bottle of whiskey and an axe."

Natalie laughed. Maura did not.

"I was kidding, little miss. That was a joke. You've heard of jokes, yes?" Maura glared at him. "This one got it." he grumbled, pointing at Natalie. "Alex, grab your grandma's bag."

It had been years since I had seen Grandma's bag, but I knew just what he meant. Grandma Jean had been a nurse. Even when she was off the clock she carried a bag of emergency medical supplies. Ace bandages, Neosporin, the material for a splint, tweezers, rubbing alcohol - the whole nine yards.

I snagged the bag from its spot beneath the bathroom sink and returned to the living room. I would be shocked if there were a child in this neighborhood who didn't know this bag. Used to be that when a kid got hurt, you brought them to Grandma Jean. Not only was she good at tending to wounds, but she was also good at cheering the child up. You always got a treat from her Cookie Monster cookie jar before you left. I wondered if Maura had ever had one of Grandma Jean's snickerdoodles. It broke my heart that Natalie never would.

Grandpa looked Natalie in the eye. "I'm gonna give it to you straight, kid. You sprained your wrist and it's gonna hurt for a few days. Today especially. I'm gonna wrap it up for you so it doesn't wiggle around and hurt any worse than it has to. But you can't use it for a while. That means no video games, and none of that stuff on the IPAD."

Natalie scowled. Grandpa James chuckled and rustled her unruly curls. "It ain't all bad. You can sit on your keester and watch TV all day if you want." This brought a smile to Nat's face.

"How do you know it's not broken?" asked Maura.

"I've seen my fair share of sprains and breaks. She's a tough kid," he said, nodding toward Natalie. "But she's not so tough that she could laugh at my jokes with broken bones. She's gonna be alright."

"Thank you," said Maura. If she still had doubts she was hiding them.

"Fire up the truck Alex! This kid needs Redbox and junk food, on the double."

Maura rolled her eyes. "Greaaaaat. Hello cabin fever."

"Better than the emergency room," sang Grandpa James.

I snagged the keys. Grandpa James rarely asked me to do anything. Besides, the way he was around Natalie reminded me what it had been like to be around him as a kid. Maybe he didn't have much left to offer the adult world, but he had something special when it came to kids. For whatever reason, he got them. In a way I wished Natalie were here all the time. I wondered if he would still drink, with little eyes around watching and worshipping him.

Natalie stayed with Grandpa while Maura and I headed to the store, courtesy of a 20-dollar bill straight from Grandpa's wallet. We stocked up on the least messy, most delicious treats available: Strawberry ice cream (Nat's fav, apparently), Red Vines, Bottle Caps, and of course diet soda, which I had come to learn was a staple in their household. The Redbox part was a little harder.

"You're seriously checking out three Barbie musicals and the Sound of Music?" I asked.

"It's what she likes."

"You're going to slit your wrists by 9pm,"

Maura laughed. "I kinda like them...."

"You have got to be kidding me! We are re-educating your sister on movie tastes...and apparently you as well."

Maura arched an eyebrow. "Just what exactly do you have in mind?"

I ran my debit card through the machine and picked my two favorite childhood movies: the first Transformers and the original Teenage Mutant Ninja Turtles.

"Those movies are for boys."

"Stop being a gender elitist! Anyone can appreciate the Turtles. Besides, I'm planning to watch these with you and I cannot watch two Barbie musicals without something appealing in between."

"Who's being a gender elitist now?" taunted Maura.

The taunting didn't bother me one bit. I had just invited myself over to a beautiful girl's house for six hours and aside from a little smart assy-ness she hadn't said no. Nothing could spoil my mood. I tossed a bag of Doritos into the cart for good measure.

"That does not qualify as a non-messy food!"

"Those are for me. The clean stuff is allllll yours."

" You know Alex, I will remember that when you reach for a Red Vine."

Scientifically, there is something arousing about a member of the opposite sex using your name in a sentence. I am not making this up. I read about it in Men's Health Magazine. One of the top twenty tips for getting a girl's attention is to use her name when you talk to her. It seemed stupid when I read it. But just now, hearing her prattle off my name so matter of factly made me feel rockstar special. She certainly had my attention. I made a mental note to find said magazine, re-read said tip list, employ tips stat!

Chapter Sixteen: Maura

At first I was nervous about spending an entire day with Alex. But as it turned out there was nothing to be nervous about. The two of us clicked. We got one another's lame jokes, passed the Doritos back and forth at appropriate intervals, etc. The silences that stretched between us had stopped feeling awkward and begun to feel natural. I wondered if this was what it was like to have a boyfriend. A real boyfriend, not like that jerk face ass clown from the 8th grade who tried to put his hand up my shirt and told everyone I was a prude because I squealed and slapped him in the face. In my defense, I was raised almost solely by a man. Dad's motto was pretty much slap first, apologize later. Besides, he had no business touching my lady parts after two weeks of inter hallway hand holding!

Things felt different with Alex. Comfortable. Maybe too comfortable? I didn't even know if he liked me that way. To him, I might just be a cool girl to make Jell-O with, someone to pass the time with before he went back to the city where things happen and people suck less. I pushed the thought out of my mind. I liked being around him. I would enjoy it while I could. Even if it didn't end in a kiss, it could still be wonderful just to know a person, right?

After Alex left and Natalie was sound asleep I made the call I had been dreading all day. Grandpa Mick picked up on the first ring.

"How's my favorite little pumpkin head?" (Grandpa Mick loved his new iPhone and the nerdy picture caller ID which, rather unfortunately, featured a picture of me dressed as a pumpkin in the 2nd grade.)

"I'm sixteen, Gramps."

"You'll always be my little pumpkin head."

"Did you get the pic I sent you this afternoon?"

"I did. How's Natalie holding up? That looked like a pretty nasty bump."

"She's fine. But it could have been worse. She could have broken her arm or something. I can't even take her to the doctor without Dad. Grandpa, I can't do this without him. I need you to tell him to come home."

"Maura, honey, you're doing fine. You can handle this. It's just a few weeks."

"Yeah well...what if I don't want to handle it? What if I'm tired of being the adult? It's my last year to be a kid, you know. He's supposed to be here." I hadn't meant to cry but suddenly the tears were flowing with a mind of their own.

"Aw honey, don't get upset. Your dad's not gone forever. I'd stay with you myself but I've got to close on our rental in Arizona, and I'm meeting your dad and uncle in a few days as it is."

I had forgotten that Grandpa and Uncle Andy were meeting Dad. Dad may not think it's kosher to bring a cell phone on a hunting trip, but Grandpa Mick never went anywhere without his phone. As a retired engineer, the man loved his technology as much if not more than he loved his own children.

"I need you to do me a favor, Gramps.'

"Name it."

"Make him call me. The second you find him make him call me. I need to say some things and they can't wait a month. Besides, an eight-year-old can't go that long without talking to her dad."

"I can try, sweetie, but you know how your dad feels about being out there. He's not going to want to bring his home life into the wilderness."

"Yeah, well, he's gonna have to suck it up. Mom hasn't called and asked for Natalie in three months. The least he can do is be the parent that bothers to call." I knew it was a mean thing to say and that it would cut Dad to the core, but it was also true. He was acting just like Mom right now. It was all about him and for the hundredth time in our lives Nat and I were second rate to someone else's ambitions. I hoped to God I never had kids. Good parents put their kids first, good parents let go of their own dreams. I didn't know if I had it in me. My own parents sure as hell didn't.

"It's just a phone call, Grandpa. Try - okay?"

"Of course. I won't just try. I'll insist. If you promise to quit the waterworks, that is."

I exaggerated a sniffle. "I can do that."

"We're headed up there Monday. We oughta make camp by 5. You can expect a call around then."

"Thank you Grandpa, it's gonna mean a lot to Natalie."

"Just Natalie, huh?"

"Both of us."

What I didn't tell Grandpa was that I had received a disturbing call today regarding Dad. It was from his doctor. Now, I'm not saying Pendleton doctors are somehow beneath the doctors in bigger towns but, well,.the whole doctor patient confidentiality bit wasn't exactly as hardcore as they made it out to be on TV. I was used to getting calls from Dr. O'Daniel typically appointment reminders for Dad, along with some subtle suggestions for me. Suggestions like, "Ease up on the high fructose corn syrup," and "Try to keep Nat quiet if your Dad's able to get any sleep." But today's call had been slightly more alarming. It seems Dad had missed an appointment. A rather important appointment. The kind of appointment he should have told his daughter about. Today was the day he was supposed to start dialysis. Now I knew that kidney failure COULD happen. In fact, I knew it happened a lot to people with diabetes. But I didn't know that it WAS happening. I didn't know that it was happening to my Dad, and I should have known. Because we don't hide things. Dialysis is expensive, and painful, and only a way to minimize symptoms. If he needed dialysis he needed a kidney, and they don't carry that sort of thing in the markdown bin at Walgreens. I didn't know if I wanted to scream at him or hug him, but both of those things would be infinitely easier if I had some fucking clue where he was.

Chapter Seventeen: Mike's Journal

To my girls.

When I was 12, my family could not be contained. Your uncle and I were natural outdoorsmen, not the Boy Scout sort, but the real sort. The kind who spent their weekends hunting, fishing, and hiking every square inch of Oregon. We were lucky because our mother was as at home in the wilderness as she was in our living room. I can't imagine what my childhood would have been like if Mom was the kind of woman who would rather stay back at camp than venture into the woods.

People used to joke that Mom and Dad were destined to spend their retired years as unshaven Sasquatch people, traveling from forest to forest, oblivious to human interaction. I didn't know exactly what retirement was at the time but I equated it to freedom. It was a great fantasy of mine, the idea that my parents might one day build a cabin in the Blue Ridge Mountains and host my brother and me for holidays and hunting trips. I liked to imagine grabbing my bow from the garage and hunting in their new backyard. I liked to think of my own sons accompanying me. As you know, retirement never came.

I've thought about it and decided there's no good reason to write about my mother's death. It wasn't complicated. It wasn't tragic. Thousands die like her every day. Reading about it wouldn't help you understand your grandmother, just like writing about it won't help me get over her.

What I will tell you is that there is no shock value with cancer. Blame the made-for-TV movies, or the thousands of books about living with and dying with cancer, but somewhere along the line you become insensitive to the disease. For me, insensitivity came early. When you're 15 and you have to carry your 86-pound mother to the toilet and back, things stop being shocking, tragedy becomes real. Becomes commonplace. Which is worse I couldn't tell you. She's dead now and that's that. I regret my life without her. I regret your life without her. If I could make you understand one thing about the whole damn situation it would be this, disease is ugly. No child should watch their parent die slowly. There are things you cannot unsee, feelings of hatred you cannot unfeel. Some part of you already knows this whether you have come to recognize it or not.

But when I was 12, before her Cancer ravaged us all, we were unstoppable. SHE was unstoppable. There must have been weekends we spent at home, but they don't stand out in my memory. What I remember is packing the Chevy, squeezing four in the cab, dirt bikes in the bed, and heading to the mountains. Sometimes we planned our trips and sometimes we found the trip along the way. No matter where the weekend took us my mother was prepared. For this reason, (and probably a thousand others) your grandfather worshiped her. We all did.

She was always good at finding great camp spots, but the day she found the lake we all knew she had found something big.

Just outside of Bend, deep in the Deschutes Forest was a small unmarked lake. It might have a name now, but then it was just a blue dot on a map. The water was so clear you could see to the bottom. Even in the deepest parts, you could see the fish and they could see you right back. We camped just inside the tree line where the forest met the sand. In the afternoon we hiked, in the evening we cooked on the camp stove. Uncle Andy and I were still young enough to beg to roast marshmallows and stay up late. You don't know this about your grandpa, but he used to tell stories. Great stories about heroes who could outrun cheetahs. The stories stopped when your grandma died. I used to think they would come back for you girls, but the time for that has come and gone. Grief, you'll soon learn, can ruin a person if you aren't careful. Don't let grief suck the joy from your life. There is so much more to feel out there than heartbreak.

Your grandpa and uncle were late risers. Mom and I, on the other hand, were always the first to wake up, always the first to set up camp. It was the seventies, and she let me drink coffee and say "dammit." I thought that made her the best mother in the world. I still believe your uncle and I were gifted with an exceptional mother. If being married to Mary-Anne taught me anything it was that motherhood isn't a given. Not every woman is a great mother. Love is truly not all it takes.

Together your grandmother and I would park our lawn chairs in the spots where the early morning sun hit the beach. Together we drank bitter camp coffee, black, because she liked it that way and I didn't dare tell her I secretly craved a little sugar.

Together we watched the animals come out of the forest and drink from the far side of the lake. Even at twelve, I knew these moments mattered. I knew they were measured, even if I didn't know just how measured.

On our last day at the lake we packed in silence, enjoying the quiet rustle of the forest, the birds in the trees, even the horse flies that buzzed dangerously close to our faces. I watched her face in the rear view mirror as we headed back to town. She was full of longing, already mourning the trip, as if she knew there would be so few more to come. I was sure we would go back there, but we never did. When I asked her why she replied, "The sure way to destroy perfect is to try and recreate it."

I know I've told you girls about the lake before. But I should have taken you. We'd have made our own new and perfect memories. I know that now. Sitting here now with the sun warming my face and your grandmother's memory for company my only real regret is never sharing her spot with you.

Your grandmother had a Catholic funeral and a Catholic burial. Her body is under a stone in Roy Raley Cemetery but when I think of my mother's final resting place, I don't think of the place we bring flowers each year. I think of the lake. To me she is here. I should have brought you here to be with her.

Chapter Eighteen: Maura

For once, I was happy to be woken up by Natalie jumping on the foot of my bed. Did I want to get up and play with her? Not particularly, but she had saved me from the dream and that was something to be grateful for. It wasn't as if it was the first time I had dreamt it. It was more the realization that for the first time, it was close to real. The dream was born of a memory; the sort of memory you shove to the back of your mind. The sort of memory too scary and unreal to store with the rest of your thoughts. In my waking hours, I tried not to think about the things that could go wrong now, the things that had gone wrong in the past, or the things that inevitably would go wrong in the future. But I had no control over the dreams. I'm not a dream psychologist or anything, but I would imagine dreaming about the night we lost Dad in the woods had a direct correlation to that call from Dr. O'Daniel.

I didn't talk to anyone about that night, not Elizabeth, not even Mom when she called to check up on us. My silence didn't change the fact that the whole town knew by morning. You couldn't even have UPS come to your house and keep it a secret in Pendleton. So try and imagine just how fast the rumors flew when we not only had an ambulance at the house, but the police department, complete with search dogs and flashlights.

The evening started like any other evening at our house. TV dinners with Alex Trebek, a bedtime story for Nat, and Dad passing out in his lazy boy. It wasn't that he was lazy, it was just that the nerve damage in his feet made it so difficult to lay down and sleep at night that he typically caught his Z's 20 minutes at a time throughout the day. He took a sleeping pill at night to help him settle down, but it was hit or miss. It seemed to be working pretty well that night because when I went to bed at 11:00, he was still out there snoring to a backdrop of bad reality TV. When I awoke two hours later, that was no longer the case. The sound of breaking glass sent both Natalie and me flying from our rooms. There stood our father, blood dripping down his right arm, his face red from exertion. At first I thought someone had broken in, but aside from the wind whistling through the broken window the house was silent. He looked at us as if we were strangers, as if nothing about us belonged to him. Natalie began to cry. I stood there dumbfounded, not sure where to begin or what to ask. He didn't give me a chance anyway. He mumbled something about demons escaping through the window, then sprinted out the back door and into the woods that surrounded our houses. I didn't want to call the police, but what else was I supposed to do? Grandpa Mick and Uncle Andy were on a fishing excursion in Alaska, and Aunt Nick already thought Dad was bottom of the totem pole. I was afraid she'd have him committed or worse.

When the police came, they asked what he had been wearing and it was then that I first realized the complete and utter absurdity that my father was running through the woods, entirely out of his mind, in nothing but boxers, a T-shirt and his tender bare diabetic feet.

I knew what the police were thinking. They thought my father was crazy. No one had to say it. I knew because in that moment *I* was deathly afraid that my father was crazy. The officer who took my report was young and healthy. He was probably the older brother of someone I knew from school. I wished he wasn't. I wished he was a hardened older man, the kind who could reassure me he had seen things like this before. The kind who could say, "No worries, chickadee. There's always a reason for these things." Instead, there was Mr. Handsome, looking around our house like evidence of crazy was strewn all over the place. After taking my report, he and the others made an initial foray into the woods. It took less than ten minutes for them to come back to my doorstep and admit that they weren't going to find him on their own. He wasn't answering to his name, and though they had heard some rustling in the bushes it was nearly impossible to locate him if he didn't want to be found. I thought that was it. That they would call protective services and haul us away because my father apparently "didn't want to be found," aka "didn't want to be a dad."

Now, I know that nothing is further from the truth, but at 14 I was scared and afraid. I was also wrong. They came back twenty minutes later with a search party and the kind of dogs I thought you only used to sniff out drugs or dead bodies. I prayed then. We weren't religious, never had been, and to tell you the truth I haven't gotten down on both knees since. But that night, I prayed those dogs would not find my father.

Either that prayer fell on deaf ears or God has a keen understanding that 14-year-olds don't always know what to ask. They did find my father, curled up in the fetal position, fast asleep on the forest floor. They said they'd never seen anything like it, that he had to have hidden in the trees to avoid them that long in the first place. And then, did he just suddenly decide to lay down and go to sleep? It didn't make sense, especially not for a person with a healthy mental history. He woke easily and was cooperative returning to the house.

He will tell you now that he doesn't remember anything about demons, can't remember punching the window, and can't even for a second understand what he was doing out there in the woods. He also doesn't remember being interviewed by the paramedics. It was they who suggested we take Dad to the hospital and see what was really going on. During the car ride to the hospital, Dad was fully lucid. Lucid enough to make jokes like: "How many squirrels do you think I ate while I was out there playing Hatchet?" and "All that hunting and animal tracking finally paid off. If the police dogs can't find me, then I'm sure as hell outwitting the deer!" It was a relief to hear him joking around.

I wanted to hate the young officer for scrutinizing my family, but on the ride to the hospital he let Natalie sit on Dad's lap in the back of the squad car. She needed her dad and I guess he was compassionate enough to see that. Sometimes when I see him around town he'll give me a half wave, just personal enough to be personal, but I never wave back. He probably thinks I'm rude but I mostly just don't like to be reminded. But there are other times I want to stop him in his tracks and tell him what the doctors said so he can stop looking at me with pity.

After about a zillion tests it was determined that Dad had actually had a major heart attack, probably in his sleep, and as a result his body had gone into some kind of shock that didn't pair well with sleeping pills and incredibly low blood sugar. Natalie knew enough about heart attacks from TV to be terrified. We couldn't seem to make her feel comfortable just with kind words and reassurances, so the three of us took a CPR class together, where we all learned to recognize the signs of a heart attack and what to do if, Heaven forbid, it ever happened again.

I didn't worry about his heart, though. That was too much. Between his diabetes and his feet, I couldn't wrap my head around yet another health concern to be afraid of. I worried about the crazy though. It was the crazy that brought my nightmares. It was the crazy that made me afraid he wasn't just hunting out there now.

Chapter Nineteen: Mike's Journal

To my girls.

I scared away the squirrels. It's not all that much of a surprise. I should have let them be, but I got so used to their company I felt like they ought to have a proper shelter. I guess it wasn't my brightest move. They've been living out here their whole lives. Why on earth should they need a padded lean-to now?

For a solid week I had company for every meal. Is it pitiful to admit that this full grown man misses his Chip and Dale? If it is, I guess I fit the bill. Don't worry, I haven't replaced you. I'm well aware that any therapist worth her salt would tell me that symbolically, the squirrels are actually you twerps.

I think about you all the time. I wonder what you're up to. If you've gotten any braver. Have you written anything lately, Maura? I tell you all the time that those stories and poems you tuck away when no one's looking, they're real good. But you don't listen. No one's ever gonna know they're good if you keep pretending they aren't worth reading. I know I've asked plenty of you in the last seven years, but I'm asking you for one more thing now: Stop being afraid that you aren't good enough. You have always been more than good enough to me. Listen when that inner voice tells you, you're destined to do big things.

I know you are afraid of ending up like her. Hear me when I tell you that wanting more than Pendleton does not make you your mother. When you doubt that remember this. The fundamental difference between you and Mary-Anne has always been your capacity to love. Your ambition does not fill the void where a heart belongs. Chase your damn dreams Maura just remember that your family is behind you every step of the way.

Chapter Twenty: Alex

Grandpa James had been unusually chipper lately. Chipper and sober. Not completely, of course, but more so than usual. I was pulling my shoes on for a walk downtown when he tossed an envelope at me from across the room.

"What's this?"

"Try opening it."

I rolled my eyes. For a secretly kind man he behaved like a total smart ass.

"Rodeo tickets?"

"Not just rodeo tickets. PBR tickets." The only PBR I knew of was Pabst Blue Ribbon, the cheapest of the cheap beer and I didn't imagine they sold 30 dollar tickets for that. Grandpa must have read the confusion in my face because he started explaining before I had a chance to ask.

"Professional Bull Riding, son. Rodeo clowns, bucking songs, the whole nine yards. Rodeo starts this week. Take your girlfriend."

My face turned four shades of red. "She's not my girlfriend."

"You told me THAT when you were five, too!"

"Grandpa!"

"Take her or don't take her, it's up to you. There're enough tickets in there for the little one and a tagalong. If you're too afraid to ask her out, you can always say it's to cheer up the wounded kid."

A smile crept across my face.

"Now that is a brilliant idea."

"I have those every now and again. Show's tomorrow night, though, so I wouldn't waste any time with the asking."

I heeded grandpa's advice. If Maura thought I was a dateless wonder, it didn't matter. You can't say no to a guy offering to take your injured baby sister out to a show. Plus, inviting her friend Elizabeth along made it feel a lot less like a date and more like an "outing." Which is how I described it to Maura, who laughed and said she would go only if I promised to never call anything an outing again.

Now, standing in front of the full length mirror on my bedroom door I was having second thoughts. Sooo many second thoughts. Second thoughts like, "Should I make a move?" "Is it pervy to make a move when she's sitting next to an eight-year-old?" and "Docs taking someone out to a show with a total value of approximately $20.00 grant you one goodnight kiss free of charge?"

Grandpa chose just that moment to walk by, take the last slug of his beer and grumble, "Standing in front of the mirror won't make you any better looking...or better dressed."

Sometimes when I was inclined to use choice words in his direction, I reminded myself that he was feeding and housing me, and tonight, fully sponsoring my date-ish thing. I did not, however, think it was wise to listen to his fashion advice, seeing as how the man wore black denim jeans with a white undershirt every day of his life. No, I was pretty sure that my blue flannel button-down with jeans would be fine. More than fine really. I would go as far as to say it looked like I had muscles in this shirt.

It was a tight squeeze in the truck with all four of us in the cab. Elizabeth and Maura chattered the whole way to the Round-Up grounds, which was fine with me because quite frankly I had been at a loss for words since Maura came down the front steps. Her blue denim skirt and white tank top left little to the imagination. Plus there was just plain something hot about cowboy boots on a girl.

Rest easy, I was NOT wearing boots. Nope, good ol' fashion Chucks were my style. Besides, whereas any girl could rock cowgirl boots, any non-ranching dude who tried came off looking like the Mayor of Douchebagistan.

Elizabeth was her usual perfectly coiffed self, filled with animated stories, lots of talking with her hands. She was not my kind of hot. But she was, in fact, the scientific definition of hot. Perfectly proportioned. A B-cup to match a tiny waist and only slightly voluptuous in the hip department. Flawless skin, dimples in each adorable cheek. Big, fat gleaming eyes and hair that made you wonder if you were also attracted to that little archery princess from Brave. She kind of defied logic. But to me? To me, hot was a smart-ass attitude, telling me Red Vines were off limits and Teenage Mutant Ninja Turtles were rotting brains left and right.

Our seats were decent. We weren't in the box with the mayor by any means, but hey, Nat could see without a booster seat so you might say Grandpa did a good job.

"How'd your grandpa score these tickets anyway?" asked Elizabeth. "They were sold out when my step-dad tried and that was a week ago."

"Funny you should ask," I replied. "I feel strongly that you will not believe me if I answer truthfully."

Maura raised an eyebrow, "Go on".

"Allegedly, he won them in a particularly harrowing round of bar trivia."

"Trivia?"

"Yeah, apparently his typical Thursday night is trivia at The Hungry Clam. And get this: He won sans any teammates. Like, he just plants himself in a corner booth and conquers the shit out of 16, 8-person teams of 21-plussers."

"I want to be shocked by that, but your grandpa is kind of ridiculously unpredictable."

"Unknowable, really."

Maura frowned. "You know your Grandpa, Alex."

"I know what my grandpa likes to drink. I know where he keeps spending cash and what he does with the boring hours of the day, and that he usually spends about 45 minutes crying and talking gibberish to Grandma Jean's high school graduation portrait each night. But it would be a stretch to say that I know him. We'd have to talk for that." No sooner were the words out of my mouth than I regretted them. We weren't here to play the therapist and the emotionally unstable teen.

Fortunately, Elizabeth broke the silence. "Well, as fun as that revelation was, they are about to shoot the cannon and start the show. Out of respect for the tight pants and soon to be flying cowboy hats, please stand, cover your heart, and enjoy what I am positive will be a terrible rendition of the national anthem."

"Terrible" didn't quite describe what happened next. Based on the smirks and giggles between Elizabeth and Maura, the teen pop wannabe currently belting out "Rockets' red glaaaaaaaaaare!" was a classmate. Somehow, she managed to make the national anthem seem like an ugly ex-boyfriend hate anthem. Taylor Swift had nothing on this chick.

When the song was over, Elizabeth did an elaborate cross-your-heart and pointed to the sky. "Praise Jesus!"

"I'm not sure Jesus and the National Anthem are involved," I snickered. But Elizabeth's attention was elsewhere. About four rows ahead of us stood an early edition Avril Lavigne fan. (If Avril got her entire wardrobe from the punkish rack at Walmart.) She too was in the cross-yourself-for-the-Lord motion, though clearly the girls found prayer more amusing than spiritual.

Combat Boots winked at Elizabeth and turned back to the show. Finally, we were permitted to sit and the lights went down.

Now, I don't know what I expected to happen here, but suddenly I was overwhelmed with fear. Straight up fear that it was my moment to make a move and I was gonna let it slip by because I'm too much of a wimp to take her God damn hand. Ahead of us, a slick-looking guy in a "made to look weathered" Metallica shirt made the old yawn move before pulling Combat Boots into cuddle position. For a tough-looking chick she all but melted onto his shoulder. That was enough. If that dude could get that girl to go for him, I could surely get Maura to hold my hand without the police streaming in to haul me away. Worst case scenario, she wasn't into it and would pull away. Best case scenario...No...I was not going to allow myself to think about that right now. Hope is a dangerous thing when it comes to women. I learned that sophomore year when I foolishly asked my senior neighbor to the prom. "You're like a little bro to me, bud." Ouch. It was still a stinger to think about. And to think of all the time I spent in her driveway rebounding her crappy jump shot so she could make varsity. Like a brother? Brothers most certainly spend their free time picturing you in your underwear.

Thinking about Sheila was not exactly bolstering my confidence. Time to tune out the past and live in the now. I subtly wiped the clammy sweat from my right hand. Maura was sitting with her legs stretched out on the seat below us, both hands resting on her lap. Perfect for taking into my own. All I had to do was inhale and swipe, inhale and swipe. I looked to Natalie for courage. Her eyes were glued to the rodeo clown skipping around in his ridiculous garb making jokes that were only funny to hillbillies. Give me a sign, Butterball, I thought. And then...it happened. Natalie laughed so hard Coke shot out of her nose. When Maura turned to scold her for spraying the couple in front of her - boom! - I saw my opportunity and grabbed that open hand! The surprise on her face was palpable. Good or bad palpable I didn't know, because at that exact moment Elizabeth flew out of her chair. "I'm not big on third-wheeling it. I'm out of here". Maura dropped my hand with far less effort than it took me to grab hers.

"I'll be right back," she mumbled before following Elizabeth down the stadium stairs and into the concession alley.

Nat wiped the remnants of soda from her cheeks. "You think my sister is hot like Leonardo thinks April ONeil is hot."

I nodded. "Something like that."

Natalie giggled. "My dad says he keeps his shot gun clean and loaded for Maura's first real boyfriend."

"You are not helping."

Nat patted me on the back in the condescending way that is only cute on a chubby eight-year-old in a splint. "If it doesn't work out you can still come over for My Little Ponies. I don't hold grudges."

Chapter Twenty-one: Maura

I'm only really stupid when I'm nervous. Which was why I was hoping Elizabeth would forgive me for acting like a total nutbag last Friday. In my defense, everything I saw happen pointed toward my theory. I mean point blank. Alex took my hand, and within 30 seconds Elizabeth was high tailing it out of the stadium. Was I totally off base to think the two were connected? At the time, it didn't feel like it. At the time, it felt a bit like Elizabeth was finally telling me she liked me a bit more than a friend. Of course that's what it would feel like IF I were the only person on the planet. Which of course was not the case.

It had been 72 hours, but her words still stung. "Did it ever occur to you that it's not always about you? You know, like, other people matter too? I don't spend all my time sitting around wondering what you're up to. Or *who* you're up to I should say. Besides, who even said I was gay? You're my best friend. You aren't supposed to believe all that bullshit."

As much as I hated to admit it, she was right about me being the center of my own universe. But honestly, aren't we all? And sure, it would have been wrong for me to assume that she was gay because everyone at school did. But that isn't why I thought that. Correction: why I know that. That isn't why I KNOW that. I know she's gay because since the third grade every crush she's had has been on a girl even if she can't say it out loud. When she didn't get invited to Analie's 11th birthday party she cried, and not because she was desperate to swim with the cool kids. No, she cried cause Analie was the prettiest girl in school and Elizabeth adored her.

I was an idiot for not figuring it out last night, but she wasn't upset because Alex held my hand. She was upset because Nikka was four rows away, head to shoulder with Nick Anderson. Had I been paying attention to more than just my ridiculous crush on Alex, I would have picked up on that. But as it was now, the moment had come and gone. Elizabeth was mad and would probably stay mad, but there was nothing I could do except say "I'm an idiot," and wait for her to come around.

My bigger concern was whether or not Alex would come around. I couldn't have slipped out of that hand-hold any faster if I were a water snake steering clear of a crocodile. The drop-off hadn't gone any better. I practically flew out of the cab of the truck dragging a reluctant and sleepy Natalie much faster than her little chubtastic legs were used to. I had heard nothing from Alex or Elizabeth all day and I was beginning to accept my life of teen loneliness when my cell buzzed on the dining room table.

I wasn't sure who I wanted it to be, Elizabeth or Alex?? If it was Alex he could be asking me out and sure, that is what rom com loving me would want. But real me? The me that has to walk, talk, and breathe found the premise just a bit terrifying! And if it were Elizabeth? Suddenly I was afraid everything I said and did came off completely self absorbed. Maybe I wasn't a good listener after all. As it was I didn't really have to worry about either as the number currently flashing across my caller ID didn't belong to either party.

Of course! Grandpa. He promised to have Dad call. I'd been so busy fixating on teenage drivel that I completely forgot today was the day that Grandpa and Uncle Andy met up with Dad! I had given this a lot of thought since Natalie sprained her wrist and I was prepared to tell Dad what he needed to hear: WE were his most important last steps. WE needed him here more than he needed the woods. More than he needed to relive childhood memories and catch that elusive last buck.

"Dad!" There was a long pause.

"I'm sorry, sweetheart, but it's still just Grandpa."

"Oh, no biggee. But can you put Dad on? I want to talk to him now before I lose my courage."

"Just a second hun. How's Natalie holding up?" It wasn't like Grandpa to make small talk. He was stalling. If Dad was refusing to talk to me, I was gonna lose my shit.

"Natalie's fine, Grandpa. Put him on."

"I want to Maura, I really do, but it's not possible right now."

"What do you mean it isn't possible? You tell him I don't give a crap whether or not talking on a cell phone disturbs his hippie romp! His kids need him, and need trumps want. Put him on the phone!"

"I want to Maura, I really do."

"Then grow a pair, Grandpa!" I had never talked to Grandpa Mick like this before but, clearly, behaving wasn't going to get me anywhere. Besides, I was angry. I had the right to be angry.

There was a heavy sigh on the other end of the line before I heard Uncle Andy's gravelly voice interrupt in the background. "Just give me the phone and I'll handle it." If Uncle Andy thought, he was going to pacify me he was out of his mind.

"Put my dad on the phone." My voice was firm, confident. I was sure that they had both underestimated my resolve.

"I can't put your dad on the phone because I don't know where your dad is."

"What?" I could feel my heart constricting, the air squeezing out of my lungs.

"I'm sorry, honey. We're still looking."

"I don't understand. You were supposed to meet him. He's supposed to be at camp."

"I know. It could still be a miscommunication. Maybe he thought we were meeting somewhere else. We're still looking, Maura. There is no need to panic."

"No need to panic!" I was angry now. "My dad is missing! My sick dad is missing and you want me not to panic? He's been gone for thirteen days. He could be hurt!"

"Your dad is a full grown man, Maura. I'm sure there's a reason he isn't here. Give us a little time and we'll call you when we know more."

"You know this could be more than miscommunication. You know that! This could be him under the house again! This could be him climbing into the trees hiding from the demons.

This could be so many things!" I knew it wouldn't help but there was nothing else to do, so I sat there sobbing into the phone.

I finally heard Grandpa Mick tell Uncle Andy to let me know they'd keep me posted, but it was senseless to stay on the phone when they had limited battery. I didn't wait for a Uncle Andy to respond before slamming the phone down. What could he say anyway? More worthless pacifying shit about how my dad was a big boy? How he knew his way around the woods? My dad struggled to walk across the living room. Forgive me, but I had zero confidence that Dad was suddenly self-sufficient.

There were only two possibilities here. Either Dad was hurt and needed my help, or Dad was planning to hurt himself. Either way, I was supposed to sit and wait? Those guys were fooling themselves if they really believed Dad forgot where they were supposed to meet. They'd met at the same camp every year since Dad and Andy were old enough to shoot a bow. He knew every inch of that place. They all did. They were terrible hunters, but wonderful explorers.

My Dad wasn't lost. There's a difference between being lost and not wanting to be found.

Chapter Twenty-two: Mike's Journal

Dear Maura,

I've never told you about the day you were born. I've thought about it often but it turns out it's hard to explain the really beautiful things. Since I can't seem to get it out in a conversation, I figured I'd try it on paper.

I was 21 the year you were born and had been in love with your mother since the third grade. She didn't feel the same way about me until puberty hit. I took her to a middle school dance and after that it was pretty much understood that she was mine and I was hers (even though we hadn't danced within 3 feet of each other the whole night).

Your mom wanted to do big and wonderful things in big and wonderful places. I wanted to open an auto-repair shop here in town. I guess you could say my ambitions weren't very ambitious, but Grandpa Mick was happy I had a plan and I figured my good luck run with your mother had been longer than I deserved in the first place. So when she told me, through the world's largest puddle of tears, that you were on the way, I figured I had won the lottery and that she would come around, just like in middle school. I was both right and wrong. She started that conversation with, "You're going to be a Dad," and ended it with, "I'm breaking up with you."

Maybe you didn't know this, but your mother and I were separated during your entire pregnancy. I would see her around town and she'd avoid me like the plague. I got a job working as a contractor's assistant just so I could give her more money. I sent her baby supplies, diapers, clothing even an old crib I scored at an estate sale for a wealthy former councilman, all sorts of junk, but she could barely look at me without getting angry. I never got to feel you kick or watch you grow. Your mother who had been my best friend and closest confidant since the third grade became just another face on the sidewalk. I wanted to be a part of your life from the moment she told me about you but I guess after so long of not hearing from her you stopped feeling real. I'm not proud of this, but I gave up trying with your mother. The last trimester we didn't so much as wave at each other in the grocery store. I was young and stupid and I reasoned with myself that if she wanted me to I would be a dad, and if she didn't want me to I would look for greener pastures, so to speak.

But then you came. It was one of our snow days. One of those days where the whole town seems to shut down. Everyplace but Great Pacific and the library was closed for inclement weather. You know me, I'm not much of a reader so I was down at the GP with my boss. The job we were on required supplies that we couldn't get with Zimmerman's closed down for the day. We were shit out of luck workwise, but making the best of it to the tune of a beer and the meat lover's supreme.

Nobody had cell phones back then, so when you decided to make your big breakthrough your Mom had to call all over town looking for me. Bill and Sarah weren't too pleased when a personal call came in over the GP landline, but once your mother told them what was going on, I guess they decided you were worth missing a few deliveries. In fact, it was Bill who drove me over to Saint Anthony's. By the time I got there the doctor was telling your mother to push and your mother was telling the doctor where he could shove it. (Imagine your mother in labor. It isn't a pretty thing).

I looked at her and she looked at me, and for the first time in months there was no anger in her eyes, just fear. She was terrified. Terrified of the birthing process, terrified of what comes after. I wasn't much better off myself, but I knew it was my job to hide all that and show her confidence. I wanted to make her believe we could do it. We could raise a family, together, we could be happy together. Mostly I wanted her to stop feeling like Pendleton was settling and to start feeling like settling down.

And then you burst into the world! Kicking and screaming, a ball of slimy red noise. My heart's never beat so fast, and I've never been so afraid of my own hands. They put you in my arms and you just went still. Stopped all that screaming and looked up at me. Everything changed in that moment. Your mother had been the center of my universe for a long time, but I knew immediately that she had been replaced. All that drive I had for making your mother want to be with me became drive for making you happy, protected, safe. You became my purpose for everything. I thought the lottery was your mother but it turned out to be you.

You girls both have this ability to reach into my pain and pull it all out, turn it into something tolerable. You have always been capable of changing my life for the better. I wanted to give that back to you and I feel like up until now I was doing pretty well. I put you in sports. I went to your band concerts and teacher conferences. I told you were pretty and smart and funny every chance I got. I took you camping and fishing. I painted your bedrooms every time you had a new favorite color, (even when those colors were ill advised). But these last few months it's just been you building me up. I can't stand long enough to cook for you. I can't climb ladders or get up and down on my knees anymore to work for you. If I have the operation, I'll need wheelchair access to get into your concerts and even then I'll have to sit in the back. You don't know this yet but my Kidney's are shot. Pretty soon I'll spend my afternoons connected to a dialysis machine and for what? Why extend the pain so I can sit in my chair a few more years? I don't want to watch your life from the cheap seats. Please try and understand that I'm doing this as much for you as for me.

These might seem like stupid and selfish reasons to quit trying, but I can think of no worse future for you or me than spending the next ten years watching me crumble. You'll never go to college, you'll never leave town, you'll never do anything big and wonderful and since I know you don't have it in you to leave while I'm here. I'm leaving for you.

Chapter Twenty-three: Alex

"Do you still wait three days to call a girl even if the date goes not so well?"

Grandpa James looked up from his morning paper. Reading the paper in the morning was a new development. He used this time primarily to get angry about the state of the world and blame the staff of the East Oregonian for all sorts of things. He liked to use phrases like "liberal bias" which I had to physically restrain myself from laughing at. Liberal bias...in a rodeo town. He had clearly never travelled far beyond Pendleton. The local paper may not have been award-winning but you really had to stretch the definition of liberal to call it biased. Case in point. Today's headlines included " Springtime brings key decisions for winter wheat" and "Community rallies to care for sick cattle".

"Are you trying to tell me that the reason you've been moping around the place like you witnessed the death of Lassie is because your date didn't go well?"

"It could have had a better ending."

Grandpa James nodded. "Did you do something stupid?"

"No."

"Did she do something stupid?"

"Of course not."

"Hm..." Grandpa took a swig of his coffee (which, by the way, didn't smell like whiskey this morning) before responding. "Maybe you did something stupid, but you don't know it."

I rolled my eyes. "You, old man, are about as helpful as a two-legged dog."

Grandpa roared. "Maybe, so, maybe so. But I did manage to snag a pretty great lady so if it's just me and you we're looking at, I'm ahead at the moment."

I would have liked to end the conversation right there and sought my advice from a more traditional source. You know, like a father or a male best friend. But seeing as how I didn't have either of those I was stuck with Grandpa, and he did have a point. Grandma Jean was the best.

"I'm gonna humor you here and assume you know what you're talking about when it comes to girls. If it was you, what would the next move be?"

"My next move would have been three nights ago. I call the move 'kissing.' "

"And if the kissing option was not available?"

"Oh, for Christ's sake!" he hollered. "Go next door and ask what you did wrong."

I sighed. "For the last time, I didn't do anything wrong!"

"Ask yourself son, if you did would you know?"

As much as I enjoyed witty banter with Grandpa, I would have much preferred to be sparring with Maura. I was going to have to suck it up and ask her what's up. Only by the time I got the courage to go next door, Maura was already out for her afternoon run. Natalie, on the other hand, was planted firmly in front of the television. Apparently, TV was her summer guardian. You couldn't fault Maura for that. She was barely old enough to take care of herself let alone another tiny human. Natalie squealed with delight when she saw me standing at the screen door.

"Do you want to come in and play? I got new Pokemon cards!"

"How can I say no to that?"

Natalie grabbed my hand and led me down the hall. "You can't, huh? They're just too awesome!"

"Agreed."

"We aren't supposed to have boys in our bedroom but I don't think you count." I had to laugh.

"Who says I don't count?"

"Me! Besides I don't want to kiss you anyway."

"I should hope not!"

"Maura might though, so if she comes home and wants to come in the bedroom you have to leave."

"What makes you think Maura wants to kiss me?"

"She's never hung out with a boy this much before. Do you want to kiss her?"

I could feel a blush rising in my cheeks. Redheads have the unhappy misfortune of not being able to hide when they get embarrassed. "I think so, maybe, but don't tell her."

Natalie giggled. "I can keep a secret, but between me and you I think she already knows!"

Natalie and Maura shared a bedroom at the end of the hall. It looked like Natalie controlled the decorating based on the number of Twilight Sparkle figurines and cotton-candy-pink paint job. There were bits of Maura in the room, but you had to look for them. Her bed was neatly made. Her nightstand held a journal (the likes of which I would have sold a limb to read), a Kindle and a framed photograph of her and Elizabeth in cross country jerseys. Where Natalie's side of the room was covered in huge colorful images, Maura's was covered in book print. There were pages from all sorts of books pinned up with highlighted passages drawing you closer. I recognized a lot of them, like Harry Potter, Pride and Prejudice, and Hatchet, but there were a lot I had never seen before. We'd never talked about books before. Standing in her room made me want to know more about her. Did she write or just read? Was she good in school or a slacker? Did she run cross country because she liked it or because Elizabeth liked it? There were a hundred things I wanted to know but was too much of a chicken to ask.

I was just about to launch into round one of a Pokemon duel when Maura came in from her run. Natalie's eyes got huge. "NO BOYS IN THE BEDROOM!" she hissed and ushered me out into the hallway before Maura could catch us in the act.

"I thought that rule didn't apply to me," I said.

Natalie shrugged. "I've gotten in trouble for less."

I was ready to pop the kid for luring me into prohibited space when I suddenly lost all feeling in my lower half. Maura was standing in the living room chugging a Diet Coke in soccer shorts and a sports bra. You know how you were supposed to feel when they showed a hot chick drinking a Coke in a commercial? I felt that way. All melty, all too good to be true.

I guess I was in this trance a bit longer than appropriate because Natalie was poking at my ribs. "Snap out of it Alex!"

In her defense I kind of had forgotten she existed. I shook the melty thoughts from my brain and willed my legs to walk. "If the bedrooms off limits, let's duel in the kitchen, " I replied.

Natalie giggled, "The bedroom is definitely off limits, Romeo."

She was lucky she was eight. If she had been one of my friends, I'd absolutely deck her for that Romeo bit, but as an eight-year-old, it was hard not to find everything she said a tiny bit adorable. She was loveable, just like her sister.

I was going to miss them both when I moved back to Portland. The not-so-fun reality of my teenage life was I didn't really have close friends. Mom remarried so frequently that there wasn't much point in laying any groundwork in the friendship department. Most of my so-called friends were nothing more than twitter feeds to me at this point. Sure, I could tell you how they felt about the Cavs beating Golden State but I couldn't tell you what foods they were allergic to or what girl they were hung up on. Getting to know people, the way I was getting to know Maura, Natalie, and even Grandpa James, was a new thing for me.

If Maura was mad at me for the other night, she didn't show it. Nat and I dueled four times over the course of the hour and in that time Maura had been friendly. Wonderful, really. She sat next to Nat and helped her make big moves without totally shattering my game. What the girls didn't know was that Husband Number Two had been a monster gamer. I had a pretty healthy collection of Pokemon cards myself at home, not that I ever broke them out anymore.

Mom's second husband, Nick, had been my favorite. He was the one who taught me not to pay any attention to the husbands. It wasn't that he was awful, it was the opposite. He was wonderful. He gave a shit where I went, what I did. He took interest in MY hobbies, he shared his with me (hence the Pokemon collection). But he also dropped off the face of the earth as soon as he and Mom started to hit the rough patch. I begged her to make it work with him but when it came down to it, neither of them really wanted to try. Even if trying would have been best for me. That's what taught me not to pay attention to them. It hurt far less when they bailed.

"For a one-armed wonder you're pretty good at this, Nat. As much as I like losing to you I've got to check in on Grandpa." I looked up at Maura. "It's dangerous leaving old men unattended."

Nat began to pout. "There's nothing to do here. I'm tired of TV. I'm even tired of the iPad!"

That got Maura's attention, "How can you be tired of the iPad? I barely let you use it."

A sheepish grin spread across Natalie's face. "Sometimes I use it when you aren't around."

Maura looked frustrated for a second but quickly the frustration turned to defeat. She looked directly at me. "I really can't blame her. This isn't how I spent the summer when I was eight. She should be camping, fishing, being pulled behind the boat in an innertube, not glued to the TV, living in solitary confinement."

I got an idea. "You're right."

"I'm right?"

"Yes, this is absolutely NOT how her summer is supposed to go. We're wasting it."

"WE?"

"We. You, me, Grandpa James - we are wasting this kid's summer. We have to do something fun immediately."

Maura cocked one eyebrow. "Just what exactly do you have in mind?"

"The falls. We should go to the falls."

"But that's on private property."

"Grandpa knows where it's at, he can draw us a map. We used to go as kids. Don't you remember?"

"Sort of."

"Sort of? It was friggin' magical when we were kids. She'll love it."

"I don't know…"

Natalie cut her off mid sentence. "YES! YES, Maura! Say yes. We have to do something summery at least once!"

"Wasn't spraining your wrist summery enough?" Natalie scowled.

"Stop being a grump!"

With much more convincing and a lot of pouting on Natalie's part, Maura agreed we could take Natalie to the falls. Grandpa did his best to draw a map, though to be honest it was a whole lot of trees and rocks, with not that many roads to follow. He assured us we could find the place so long as we turned right at the reservation market and left when we saw a dirt road with a "No Trespassing" sign. How many grandpas draw their grandchildren maps directing them to turn on roads marked, "No Trespassing"? My grandpa had his hang -ups but he was one of a kind, that's for certain. I wondered if Mom had ever been to the falls with Grandpa James and Grandma Jean. It was hard to imagine her and Aunt Rina out braving the wilderness. But it was also hard to imagine Grandma Jean putting up with the two of them.

It turned out I didn't even have to use the map. As soon as we pulled out of Pendleton and onto the reservation, Maura told me where to turn and when to swerve for potholes. To say that she had been here before was an understatement. She had both the drive and the hike in permanently ingrained in her memory. I figured now was as good a time as any to start asking personal questions, so for once I sucked it up and said what I was thinking. "You come here pretty often then?"

Maura bit the inside of her cheek. "I used to come here often. We used to, actually," she said, looking down to where Natalie stood between us.

Somewhere along the walk in toward the falls Natalie had taken to holding both of our hands. It felt right, so right I hadn't really noticed until this moment. Now, it brought a blush to my cheeks. This was looking a lot like boyfriend, girlfriend behavior.

"I don't remember coming here," said Natalie. "You wouldn't," replied Maura. "It was when you were little. Littler, that is." She looked up from Natalie to meet my eyes. "We used to come here with my Mom and Dad, when she still lived with us. I guess they hung out here a lot in the beginning, when they were in school."

"Your parents went to school here?"

Maura laughed. "My parents did everything here. My Dad's never left here. They fell in love in middle school. They didn't know any better."

"You think that's a bad thing?"

Maura paused to think before responding. "I think it was bad for them. For one of them at least. She wanted a little bit more than he did. It just made everything ugly when they split. That's all. It's not like I don't believe in love. It's not like I think staying in one place is a bad thing. I might stay in one place, too. I'm just not sure it's here."

"If not here then where?"

"That's the hard part, right? What about you? Where are you gonna go when school starts up?"

"I'm thinking about Pendleton High School."

Maura's eyebrows shot to the sky. Until that moment I hadn't even admitted to myself how much I hoped Grandpa

James would let me finish out my senior year with him. It felt silly to say it out loud when it was still just a hope and a prayer.

"We would like it if you did," said Natalie.

"You would, eh?" I asked motioning toward Maura.

"We would," said Maura.

And maybe I imagined it or maybe the universe was starting to spin in my direction, but I was pretty sure she held my gaze just a moment too long to be considered just friends anymore.

Chapter Twenty-four: Maura

The falls never changed. They were always borderline magical. One moment you were walking through the trees and dried grass, the next you were rounding the corner on this beautiful pool of water swirling at the base of a half dozen rocks, water cascading over them just enough to glitter in the sun, just enough to make you feel like Disney movies had nothing on the reservation. Today we were alone. Usually on a hot day the falls were crowded with unattended children and lovers but today, for whatever reason, it was just us. If it weren't for the squirming eight-year-old peeling herself out of my grasp to beat us to the rocks, you might confuse this with some kind of a date. Some kind of awesome date. Some kind of date that made you feel guilty for judging people who fell in love here and never left. I knew I should be careful. But careful didn't feel as good as that flutter in my chest.

The water wasn't too cold. The August sun had warmed the pool, a benefit of it being shallow. Another benefit was that Nat could pretty much play unattended despite the fact that she wasn't a strong swimmer. There was a current, but it was only strong enough to be fun, not strong enough to pull you down river. We sat on the upper rocks with our legs dangling in the pool beneath us. Below us, Natalie lay flat on her back. Floating at peace while the water pulled her in a gentle circle. Her eyes were on the sky. What she was thinking about was beyond me, But she looked supremely happy, supremely relaxed. Alex had been right to bring her here. She needed something summery to help her forget what made this year so different. I wanted to remind her not to paddle too hard with her bad wrist, but something in the peace and quiet told me she'd figure it out on her own.

Beside me, Alex peeled the shirt from his back. "We can go in too you know."

I smiled. "I don't want to interrupt the flow. Wake the beast - that sort of thing."

Natalie's eyes popped open. "Who you callin' a beast?"

The both of us laughed. "I see what you mean," said Alex. "If it's all the same to you, I plan to lay back and get a tan."

"Don't you mean a burn?"

Alex grimaced. "There is no amount of sunscreen to protect the ginger population. We live, we burn, we accept this."

I smiled. "So long as you know this."

Together we lay back, letting the warm rock work its magic on our newly bare skin. My tankini left a lot to the imagination. Like, a lot...like all of it, which made it easier to relax around Alex. Sure, at seventeen I was old enough to get physical with a guy, but that didn't mean I was ready for it. And I was not ready for it. I was terrified of it. My swimsuit was carefully selected armor, and the fact that Alex hadn't made any dumb remarks akin to "Maura Ingalls Wilder" made me feel like maybe, just maybe, he wasn't running toward home base either.

I thought about what had happened at PBR. The hand hold that led to so much awkwardness. It was Elizabeth who took the moment from romantic to tragic, but I didn't exactly do anything to stop it or make any effort towards amends. Maybe I was still afraid then. Maybe I was still functioning like eighth-grade-Maura, ready to slap and ask questions later. Maybe I was afraid of ending up like my mother, saddled with a baby, constantly looking for a way out. Maybe that was me a week ago, but now? Now I felt a lot more like my Dad. Happy to be here, ready to love here. I slowly moved my hand across the rock to where Alex's lay open and waiting.

Chapter Twenty-five: Maura

If it was possible to be in a happiness coma I was in it, on a Monday of all days, in the morning of all times. Nothing could bother me, not Nat's incessant whining, not the cluster of bugs that met their end on my shirt during this morning's run. I was in a post hand-holding period of glee and it could not be destroyed. Or so I thought. Until we got the call.

It had been three days since Grandpa and Uncle Andy had begun looking for Dad and each night they called to say they were still looking and not to worry because things looked good. They were certain it was a miscommunication and that by the time they found Dad he would only be pissed they were late. But today's call was different. Today Grandpa Mick and Uncle Andy were on their way home, and they weren't bringing Dad with them. Because truth was, there hadn't been a single sign of Dad out there.

They told me it was my responsibility not to worry, to stay strong for Natalie. To let them handle it. But it had been a week since they started handling it and I was still further from my father than I'd ever been. I knew what needed to be done: I was going out there to find him myself. Even though I had very few outdoors skills and no sense of direction. If Grandpa and Uncle Andy couldn't find him it meant one thing. They were looking in the wrong place. Nobody knew Daddy the way I did. I would find him even if I didn't know what to look for.

I packed the essentials right away. Clothing, water, my hiking pack. The trouble was, most of the good stuff was already with Dad. I was going to have to scrounge through the attic if I wanted to go out there well prepared. I made a list of must finds.

1.Tent, True, it was only a thin sheet of fabric protecting me from the elements but I would rather hide from a bear in a tent than not in one.

2.Kerosene lamp. I hadn't learned much over the years camping with Dad, but we never went out there without a lamp so it seemed important.

3.Sleeping bags

4.Tarp. I didn't even like the idea of packing a tarp. Packing a tarp was for surviving the rain. I so did not want to be camping sans Dad in the rain.

I hadn't been in the attic since I was a kid. I had the incredible misfortune of reading a local news story about a transient who successfully lived in a local attic, unbeknownst to the homeowners, for upwards of three years. Even though NOT going into the attic was a sure way of NOT finding a stowaway, I would so much rather go on not knowing then investigate. Desperate times called for desperate measures, however, and putting childhood fears aside I had to go up there.

I made sure that Natalie was sufficiently distracted before I went into Dad's room and found the pull cord that opened the ceiling panel and brought down an ancient set of man-made stairs. I assumed no one used the attic, but clearly Dad had been up recently because his footprints were still visible in the mass of dust that accumulated on each step. I climbed the stairs with caution, careful to overstep the fourth stair, which hadn't been right since Mom tried to take the old shower insert upstairs without assistance. What was it about attics that made people store their worthless garbage up there instead of just heading to the dump?

There were loads of boxes to go through, some of them covered in dust so thick you could write your name in it. Most of the stuff was Mom's. I didn't bother going through that. She wasn't dead, just gone, no sense in getting nostalgic over someone who didn't want you.

The thing about Dad was, he wasn't organized. Nothing was clearly labeled and the boxes that were labeled weren't necessarily full of what the box claimed. Still, it didn't take long to locate a lamp and extra sleeping bag, and I was able to find a pair of Mom's old hiking boots in with the fishing nets. But I was still out of luck with the tarp. I could borrow one from next door if I had to. The only problem with that was it meant telling Alex where I was going and I wasn't looking forward to that.

I was on my way back down when a box in the corner caught my eye. It wasn't covered in dust like the rest, in fact based on the condition it had to have been put up here recently. This one was labeled and the label took my breath away. In big bold handwriting, Dad had written "Mom" across the top. My real grandma died before I was born. She died before Dad and Uncle Andy finished high school. Dad talked about her, but not a ton. He kept a photo of her on the desk in his office. Everyone says I look just like her but I don't see it. She had long dark hair that came down to her waist and she was the perfect kind of thin - not too bony, just delicate. In the picture, she was in a one-piece swimsuit with a bandana tied around her hair, sitting on the bow of Grandpa's boat. She smiled without teeth, showing perfect lips. Only people with perfect lips look good when they smile without teeth. I admired that picture when I was little, but Dad said she was already sick then and not her best. I wondered why he framed it if that was the case, but you never know what makes people do the things they do. He liked something about it. I liked that she wasn't afraid to be ghastly pale in her swimsuit. I liked that she had cancer and was still holding a cigarette.

I popped the lid off the banker's box. Inside was a scrapbook of sorts. It wasn't like scrapbooks today, all pretty, with photo squares and picture corners to hold things in the right place. This one was put together with care, but it looked like the whole thing had been done with Elmer's glue and a Bic pen. There was no image on the cover, just deep brown leather that had been handled a great many times. The pages inside were made of sturdy parchment that had begun to yellow with age along the edges. There was a dedication scrawled on the inside cover. "To Mike, Love Mom," and a photo of the two of them pasted below. My father was a baby. I'd seen a half dozen pictures of Dad in his youth, family photos mostly, the kind you pay people to take, and a few shots from out hunting with Grandpa Mick. But I'd never seen my dad as a bonafide, chubby-cheeked baby. He was sitting on his mother's lap, blond hair in disarray, coveralls too tight for his chunky frame, with the biggest smile for the camera. Grandma wasn't looking at the camera, she was smiling at her baby like she couldn't believe the wonder of it all, like making him had been some kind of perfect accident. I wondered if my mother ever looked at me that way.

It was clear this was a "Goodbye and don't forget me" book, but it wasn't depressing. There were favorite recipes with notes in the margins: "How to make Grandma's lasagna, sub cottage cheese for ricotta," etc. etc. There were photos of Dad and Uncle Andy holding various sizes of fish, antler horns, and even some potato bugs in the earlier years. There were God-awful drawings, report cards, and school photos covering years at a time. All with cute messages to remind him why they were there in the first place. "You deserved an A. I don't care what Mrs. Nana says."

And then there it was. The thing I was looking for before I even knew I was looking. A photo of Dad and Grandma in jeans and flannel, steaming coffee cups in their hands and a lake - The Lake - behind them. I'd heard about the lake a dozen times if I'd heard it once. It was special to my Dad because it was the last trip he remembered with his mom that she wasn't sick, and because they never went back. The memory was perfect, untainted by disappointment and all the other human errors. If my father had gone somewhere to get away from it all, it was here. He'd have gone looking for that lake. I knew it, the same way I knew he'd never walk Natalie down the aisle or get over my mother. What I didn't know was how to find it.

Chapter Twenty-six: Alex

What's the word for that feeling of insurmountable awesomeness that occurs when you know for certain that the girl you'd give a kidney to get to like you, so obviously does like you? Whatever that word is, that is what I was feeling. There are a lot of crossed signals a guy can get but when SHE takes YOUR hand, all the questioning goes out the window. If Taylor Swift had been standing in my living room then, I would have had the stones to ask her out. Red hair and awkwardness be damned, that day I had the confidence to move mountains.

Even grandpa James could tell a shift had occurred. "So, you're just cleaning the house then? Just polishing the furniture? Giving the windows a nice scrub?"

"I figured it was the least I could do, you housing me all summer and all."

"Mmmhmm...nothing special going on? No one special coming over?"

"No Grandpa, I'm legit just being nice."

"You'll have to forgive my being unfamiliar with the concept. You see, usually this type of action is followed up with the asking of a favor."

"Not today! Just enjoy the spoils of my good mood while it lasts."

Grandpa James took a seat on the sofa, propping his feet up on the coffee table and cracking open his first beer of the day. (Impressive considering it was already well past noon.) "I will do just that."

You couldn't wipe the smile from my face. Not even with the mud from Grandpa James boots leaving a trail of dirt clods on the floor I had just finished mopping.

Hearing a knock at the screen door. Grandpa James let loose a wry smile. "No one coming over eh? No particular reason for cleaning, just being nice you said."

A blush rose to my cheeks. "I wasn't expecting anyone."

"Sure, sure. Do you think you'll let her in or maybe just stand there like an idiot and make small talk with the old fart you live with?"

I tossed my dirty dust cloth at Grandpa and headed to the front door. Maura, visibly agitated, was pacing the length of our front porch. Uh oh! I'd seen this look on girls before. It was usually after a party where I thought everything went great but apparently was just too dense to realize I was being used. It's amazing how often girls will call you a mistake without even the slightest inkling of guilt. If I were the one on Maura's porch, telling her that crossing the great divide between friends and more than friends had been a "mistake," she would be throwing things in the general direction of my head. Any girl would. I had half a mind to stop her from starting the conversation, just tell her up front she was being a real douche bag, but thing was, she happened to be looking particularly beautiful at that moment.

Even for someone who was probably about to spew forth mean things.

She was in cut-offs with the Walmart version of Tom's and a T-shirt that read "Can We Just Not?" I, on the other hand, was in pajama pants and a wife beater, not because I'm a slob but because I'd been cleaning all morning and there was no sense making a mess of clean clothes just to change out of them anyway. As if reading my mind, she finally noticed my arrival.

"Did I wake you up?" I ran my fingers through my uncombed, uncapped hair. Maybe it would be better if I pretended I had been asleep. Then maybe there would be a good excuse for the rather unfortunate state of the top of my head.

"Naw, I've been picking up, organizing, sanitizing, etc. It's uh..it can get gross in there." Maura peeked her head in the screen door.

"It looks nice today."

"Thanks." We stood there for a moment in silence. Her hair doing that wooshy wind thing that makes men unable to form sentences.

"Did you want to come in or something? Sit down?" Maura took a seat on the front step, folding her arms over her chest and staring at the cracks in the wood. I took the spot beside her. This was more awkward than I could have anticipated. I kinda wanted to yell get it over with, but a little part of me still held onto hope. Like maybe her grandma died or something else terrible for her, but better for me.

"My dad's gone." I wasn't expecting that.

"Yeah, well...we already knew that though, right?" She looked up from the ground meeting my gaze for the first time since I'd opened the door.

"No, like, he's gone gone. My grandpa and uncle were supposed to meet him but he wasn't where he was supposed to be."

"Shit."

"Big time shit. It's been 17 days since he left and he isn't where he promised he would be."

"I don't exactly know what to say." Maura wiped a tear from the corner of her eye. "I wouldn't be over here, whining about this..." I put my arm around her shoulder, drawing her head to my chest.

"You aren't whining."

"It's just, I have to find him. I can't do this alone. Watch Natalie, graduate high school, any of it. I need my Dad, Alex."

I'd never had a Dad worth needing, but everything I'd heard from Natalie and Maura about Mike made me believe that he was the type of father who really earned it when his children said they needed him. "What are we going to do?

"We?" With my arm still slung around her shoulder I took her hand into my own.

"I kind of figured we're a we now." Maura smiled through her tears.

"We go find my father."

Chapter Twenty-seven: Alex

I figured it was best to send Maura home before I talked to Grandpa. He was a flexible guy. For the most part he hadn't asked me NOT to do anything all summer. But there was a difference between pilfering a beer now and then and taking a girl into the woods for an unspecified amount of time. I had to be delicate in my approach. Especially since taking Natalie with us wasn't an option, and neither Maura nor I knew anyone else in town who would be willing to watch the kid without asking too many questions.

I found him on the couch in the same position I left him, well, nearly the same, but not entirely. He had managed to construct a ham and Wonder Bread sandwich, heavy on the mayo, mustard and Grandma Jean's canned pickles. Grandma Jean had a fruit room in the basement where she used to store all of her canned goods. When I was a kid it was stocked with peaches, pears, and every wild berry jam you could imagine. Now it was just row after row of pickles and tuna. Grandma was a smart lady. She knew there was no sense canning things Grandpa wouldn't eat when he was the only one left to eat them. To a normal person a room full of pickles might seem odd, but to Grandma Jean it was just part of what she signed up for. Grandpa hadn't had a sandwich or a burger without one of Grandma Jean's pickles on it since the first time she had him over to her parents for dinner. He was fond of telling people "I liked her all right before the pickles, but it was the condiment selection that made me get a ring."

Schooled in the art of sucking up, I grabbed a beer from the fridge, popped the lid and handed it over to Grandpa. He looked up from his sandwich in surprise.

"Now I suppose you'll be wanting something?"

I took a deep breath. "I need your help with something."

Grandpa sat up straight, placed his sandwich on the plate beside him and gave his knee a hearty pat. "Let's hear it then."

"The girls next door are in trouble and we need to help them."

"What kind of trouble?"

"Mike's not where he said he was. Their uncle and grandpa were supposed to meet up with him for the last two weeks of the hunting trip, but when they got out there, there was no sign of him."

"Shit."

"Big time shit."

"How are we going to help with that? Not sure if you've noticed, but I don't leave the house much. I can't exactly see myself traipsing through the wilderness on a rescue mission with three kids in tow."

"We aren't asking you to."

"What exactly are you asking me to do?"

"I want you to let me take the truck and Maura so that we can look for Mike."

"That's asking quite a bit considering your mother asked me to take care of you this summer."

"Grandpa, let's be real here. Mom didn't ask you to take care of me for my well being. She asked you to take the burden off her so she can spend time with Husband Number Four. And if we are being really real, she's hoping you'll bond with me and put us in your will."

Grandpa let out a laugh. "Let's get a few things straight here. First, YOU are already in my will. Second, I'm not planning to die anytime soon and third, her burden is my blessing. It's a shame she doesn't see it that way."

"I...thank you?"

"Thank me when I'm dead. That being said though, Alex, I'm not too keen on sending you out there alone with a girl. If you do find Mike and he catches you out there unsupervised with his daughter, you are gonna be the one who needs a will."

"I'll risk it. Besides, if I don't do this she's never gonna talk to me again anyway. It's her Dad. If you've got a good one you don't give them up, right?"

Grandpa smiled. "I wouldn't know. My dad was an asshole, but Mike isn't. A little off at times, but a good guy. You can take the truck and I'll give you some money, but only for three days. If you aren't back in three days, I will report you missing and Child Protective Services will be next door a hell of a lost faster than you can ask forgiveness."

"There's something else."

"I was afraid of that."

"We need you to watch Natalie."

Grandpa growled. "Do these kids not have anyone else? What about the grandpa and uncle? Why can't they watch the chubby one?"

"Because...well, they don't know we're going and I don't think they would let us if they did."

"That sounds like a good reason for you NOT to go, Alex."

"I need you to trust me. Just for three days. If we don't find him by then, we'll come back. I promise. But we can't not try. If it was Grandma Jean, you'd have tried, right?"

"I knew your grandmother an awful lot longer than you've known Maura."

"Look, I don't know if she's my Grandma Jean yet, or just a girl I hung out with the summer between 17 and 18. But this is how I find out, right?"

Grandpa let out an exasperated sigh. "I'll do this for you. But I want something in return."

"Anything!"

"I want you to stick around. Go to school here in the fall. I've got room for you and nothing but time to spend. Your mother won't bat an eye. I know it's not Portland. We don't have all that vegetarian crap you like, but Pendleton was a good place when your mother was growing up, and it's a good place now."

I stopped him in the middle of his tirade. "Yes."

"Yes what?"

"Yes, I want to stay here with you. I've been wanting to stay; I just didn't know if the feeling was mutual."

Grandpa's face lit up with relief. Had he really thought I'd say no?" I want ya, kid. Having you around reminded me how nice it is not to be alone. I don't think I could go back to that."

"You won't have to."

"Yeah well, I don't want to raise you and your unplanned spawn, either. That's not part of the deal so please take my advice when I say it would be best if you "prepare" for your trip. If you know what I mean."

I rolled my eyes. "I'm not going to have sex."

"Uh huh. They all say that. But how do you know Maura isn't up for it?"

My face turned about six shades of purple. "I don't know that she isn't. But I wasn't going to try."

"Uh huh. And if she tries?"

"Grandpa!"

"You're my responsibility now. I have to say these things. It's my job."

"Jesus. It has literally been five minutes. Could you not save the birds and the bees for a few days down the road?"

"A few days down the road you will be cohabitating with a teenage girl, unsupervised. NOW is the time."

"I promise you, I won't have sex. Is that good enough?"

"No. Promise me you won't have sex and then take a condom just in case you're bad at keeping your promise."

"Grandpa, I'm gonna go now."

"Where?"

"Anywhere but this conversation."

Chapter Twenty-eight: Maura

Elizabeth's youngest sister answered the door. Nelly, like Elizabeth, was mostly curls. She hadn't learned to tame the beast yet. Which meant most of Pendleton couldn't tell you what color her eyes were. They were always shrouded in a curtain of curl.

"Did you bring Natalie?!" she squealed.

"Not this time babe. But I'll bring her over to play next week I promise."

Nelly scowled.

"It's not fair that Elizabeth gets to have two friends over and I get none."

"Two?"

"Yeah, her new friend Nikka is here. She's always here." Her eyes got real big. "You might be replaced now, Maura!"

I let out a tiny laugh. It was the first time I'd laughed since Grandpa called.

"I'll take my chances."

Elizabeth's room was down the hall and to the left. She was the only Adaire sister not to have to share a room. Perks of being the oldest, I suppose. Whereas Nelly and Kate's room looked like a tornado hit it, Elizabeth's was always in immaculate condition. Usually I would pop right in but seeing as how I didn't know exactly where we stood friendship-wise *and* she apparently had company, I knocked.

"Come in!" yelled Elizabeth.

I opened the door slowly, sure to let the both of them know I wasn't just another one of the siblings. I figured of the two, it would be Nikka that wore the blush, but it was Elizabeth who seemed embarrassed to see me.

"You guys probably need to chat mano a mano. I'll be in the kitchen." said Nikka, scooting off the bed and heading for the door.

I stepped to the side to let her go by. I'd never really thought about being a lesbian before. Were girls who liked girls attracted to the same thing as guys who liked girls? Nikka seemed an odd choice to me. She was basically punk, even though punk wasn't much of a thing anymore. She never came to school without combat boots and eye-liner so thick she looked like the main character in a vampire manga. Even her hair was odd. She kept it long on one side but shaved it halfway up the side on the other. My guess was she liked it that way because it showed off the roughly gazillion piercings she wore in her left ear. Her purse was one big ball of keychains and souvenir buttons, so I could hear her jingle the entire way down the hall. How funny that I noticed all this now, when Nikka had been in the same school as me since the first grade. The thing was, we didn't really hang in the same circles. Her friends got in trouble for reeking of pot after lunch break. My friends got in trouble for making out in the band practice room. There was a notable difference between my people and her people. Elizabeth, on the other hand, was a chameleon. She could fit in anywhere with anyone. If she really liked Nikka, she wouldn't bat an eye before transforming herself into one of them.

Elizabeth patted the seat beside her. "I'm sorry for being a jerk after the rodeo." That took me by surprise.

"You were being a jerk? I'm the one who made stupid assumptions." Elizabeth laughed.

"You did make a pretty stupid assumption. But that's not why I got mad at you."

"Why did you get mad at me then?" I asked.

"Honestly?"

"Of course."

"You never called me gay before. I just didn't know what to say. I didn't want to lie to you and say I wasn't, but I didn't want to talk about it either. I didn't like how you said it, like you've always known it, like it was both a fact and a secret."

"It can be both, can't it?"

Elizabeth shrugged. "I guess so."

"I'm sorry, Elizabeth. I'm sorry I acted that way. We should have had this conversation a long time ago. At a sleepover in grade school, for Christ's sake, it's not like there weren't opportunities. I just figured you didn't want me to know the same way you didn't want anyone else to know."

"I don't really think I wanted myself to know." Said Elizabeth.

"Nothing's different now. You know that, right? Nothing has to change about us." Elizabeth looked sad.

"No, nothing has to change about us. But a lot has to change about me. Nikka's not afraid to say she likes girls. She's never been afraid to say it. But I am. I'm terrified." I put my hand in hers.

"You can take your time you know."

She wiped a tear from the corner of her eye with the oversized hoodie that had become like a second set of skin to her. I couldn't remember the last time I'd seen Elizabeth at home with out that Beaver logo emblazoned across her chest. "What if she doesn't want to wait?"

"Then I guess she isn't good enough for you." Elizabeth rolled her eyes.

"Thanks Dr. Phil."

"I mean it." I said. " If she really likes you, she'll get it. Otherwise, it's kind of a waste of your time anyway."

"Maybe..."

"Definitely."

"So why'd you come over?" She asked. That was the thing about Elizabeth. She wasn't afraid to come right out and ask you things. She didn't exactly shy away from the curious stuff.

"I missed you." I said. Elizabeth bit the corner of her lip, rightfully skeptical.

"Yeah, but why now? It's been a week of silence."

"About that." I replied. " I felt dumb and I didn't know what to say."

"Right, and perhaps you were a bit distracted?" She hinted.

"Maybe, like, a lot distracted." I admitted.

"Uh huh, I figured. What do you like about him? You haven't told me anything."

"All the things. So far I like all the things." Elizabeth slugged me in the arm.

"That's not very descriptive."

"It's true though. So far there aren't any things I DON'T like. But that's not why I came over today. I wish I could say I came over here for the sole purpose of fixing things between us, and talking about boys...or girls...cuz apparently that's a thing now, but the truth is I need your help."

"Name it."

"I'm leaving town for a few days and I need someone to check up on Natalie."

"Maura! You can't leave Natalie alone for a few days!"

"I'm not, she's staying next door with Alex's Grandpa. My dad asked him to watch us this summer." Elizabeth didn't seem to like that answer. Being the oldest in her own family she knew all too well that Natalie was my responsibility.

"If you trust him to watch her, why do you need me to check up on them?"

"It's not that I don't trust him per se, it just makes me nervous leaving her over there. He drinks a lot, less lately, but still."

"Why can't Alex keep an eye on her?"

"Yeah, that's the thing. Alex is sort of going with me."

"What the hell, Maura? You've known this guy like, two weeks."

"Technically I've known him since I was five." I quipped. Elizabeth was not amused.

"You know what I mean."

I fixed my eyes on the autographed Pro Bull Riding photo across the room.

"I don't have a lot of options. I have to go and he offered to go with me. He has a truck. There isn't anyone else I can ask. If I ask anyone else, they'd wonder why my dad can't take me. You and Alex are the only two who know what's going on."

"Apparently I don't." Growled Elizabeth, "Where the hell are you going and why?"

I took a deep breath. The last thing I wanted to do was burst into tears the way I had with Alex but I could already feel their salty existence pooling up to fall.

"Grandpa Mick and Uncle Andy can't find Dad. He's been out there for more than two weeks. They spent three days looking for him. I have to find him."

Elizabeth was always popping her knuckles when she was nervous about a test or uncomfortable with a conversation. Beside me, she was methodically popping her way through her right hand. Usually Elizabeth was quick to tell you exactly what she was thinking. Not this time. This time she held back, choosing her words with great precision.

"Maura, what if there's a reason they can't find him? What if it's like before and he doesn't want to be found?" I didn't have to choose my words so carefully. I'd had a lot of time to think about this lately. I knew what had to be done.

"I'm not a kid anymore. If he doesn't want to come out from under the house, then this time it's my turn to go down and get him."

Chapter Twenty-nine: Alex

We packed the truck bed with all the necessary search party accoutrements. A tent for two (the thought of which made me so anxious I could hurl), plenty of food and water, flashlights, stuff to start a fire, a portable GPS checked out from the library in case our phones didn't get service, and a stack of playlists Maura made just for the drive. The truck didn't have a CD player or an auxiliary port so instead we rigged up one of those crazy cassette contraptions where the tape goes into the truck and then a cord from the tape connects to your Discman. The fact that Maura had both the cassette adaptor and a Discman on hand told me a lot about where Pendleton was technology-wise.

I did not pack the condoms Grandpa not so subtly stuffed in my wallet. It wasn't that I don't believe in safe sex. No, it was the fact that despite what Grandpa said about what Maura may or may not like to do, the truth was I wasn't ready to have sex. Sure, I wanted to. All sixteen-year-old boys want to, and when it happened I liked to think it would be with Maura or someone I liked just as much, but truthfully we barely knew each other. The last thing I wanted was to end up like my mother, having a baby as a teenager and then resenting it for the rest of my life. I'd always known I was unwanted, always an inconvenience. I didn't want to risk doing that to a kid, or to Maura for that matter. She hadn't explicitly said it, but she didn't have to. I knew she wanted to do more with her life than hang back in Pendleton and take care of Natalie and her father. We weren't just looking for Mike because they missed him and he ought to go home. We were looking for Mike because without him Maura was trapped.

I thought about all this as I waited for Maura to finish saying her goodbyes to Grandpa James and Natalie. As expected, Natalie was a ball of tears. In the last two days, she'd begged to go with us more times than I could count, but Maura held firm. Natalie would stay with Grandpa James. We knew what we were looking for but we didn't know what we would find. We couldn't risk bringing Natalie out there when there was a chance we'd find Mike in bad condition or, worse, not find him at all. With one final hug, Maura let go of Natalie and plopped on the seat beside me.

Grandpa James ambled up to the driver's side window. Crossing his arms and leaning on the window sill he issued his final warning. "Three days. You get three days. Not a moment longer. If you aren't home by 2pm in three days, I'll have no choice but to call the police and start a search party for all three of you. Are we understood?"

Maura nodded, "We'll all be back in three days. ALL of us. I promise."

I pretended not to notice the tears rolling down Maura's cheeks as we pulled out of the driveway, leaving Natalie and Grandpa to grow smaller and smaller in the rearview mirror. Though we didn't know our exact destination, Maura had a pretty good idea what direction to head in. The lake we were looking for was part of the Cascade Lakes that were roughly an hour outside of Bend. Total drive time was estimated at 5 hours. Finding the lake cluster wasn't going to be a challenge. Siri could get us there, no problem. The real issue was figuring out which lake was the one Mike's mom took him to as a kid. We had some clues. Last night Maura called her Grandpa to poke around for information. It hadn't been easy, subtly bringing up the lake without making it abundantly clear that we were planning to head out there, but she had managed to get some details. We knew, for example, that there were no tourist attractions there, which ruled out several of the bigger lakes. We knew they stopped to swim at Frog Lake on the way back, which meant we had to pass Frog Lake to get wherever we were going. Most importantly, we knew there was a 6-mile trail around the lake that had been well marked in 1973. If we could find the lake with the well-marked trail it was only a matter of trial and error finding the campsite. It was what we would do once we found the campsite that left me with an uneasy feeling in my stomach.

The drive from Pendleton to Bend took us through mostly desert. It was one brown mile after another, cows on the sidelines, goats on the hills, nothing particularly interesting to look at save for the girl beside me. Grandpa's truck didn't have air conditioning so we rode with the music up and the windows down. Maura kept pulling at her hair, trying to keep it from getting mussed in the wind. I didn't dare tell her how much I liked watching it fly around her face. She kept her feet on the dashboard as we drove. A summer's worth of sunshine and early morning runs made it hard to keep my eyes on the road instead of the stellar set of track legs just two feet over.

If Maura could hear what I was thinking, she'd roll her eyes. All girls roll their eyes when you try and tell them they're pretty. It's like some cruel prank from God, making teenage girls completely oblivious to the things that are good about them. I've never met a nice girl who wasn't practically crippled by insecurity. Sure, I've met plenty of not-so-nice girls who understood their looks could be a passport to getting what they want, but those girls were a dime a dozen. It didn't take long for me to wise up to the fact that what they wanted from me wasn't time and affection but objects and praise. I wanted to tell Maura how different she was from any girl I'd met before. I wanted to tell her she made it hard to function, hard to think, hard to speak, and all for good reasons. Instead I stole looks in her direction every now and again, silently hoping she could both read my mind and be flattered by it.

We didn't talk much for the first hour or so. It wasn't till we hit the town of Shaniko that Maura insisted we stop for food and a bathroom break. Shaniko might actually have the distinction of being the smallest town I've ever been to. With a population of 30 (you read that right), driving up to Shaniko felt like driving onto the set of an old western movie. People milled around here and there but mostly the town was deserted. I looked around for resident homes, but all that was left of Shaniko were the storefronts of used-to-be businesses that were now used solely for historical purposes. Our plan was to grab lunch at a diner, but there weren't any around as far as I could see.

"I'd still like to get out and my stretch my legs for a bit. What do you say to a 'ghost tour'?" I asked.

Maura laughed. "You do realize that ghost town doesn't actually have anything to do with ghosts, right?"

"Seems like a misleading name."

"It means no one lives here."

"Actually," came an unfamiliar voice. "There are three types of ghost towns." A man in brown slacks, a white button down, and old fashioned suspenders stepped out from the screen door of a small office marked Chamber of Commerce. "There are towns that are completely uninhabited but the infrastructure remains, towns that are only known as ghost towns because people remember that a town once resided there, and places like Shaniko where the population has mostly moved on but some residents remain. Technically, we are an inhabited ghost town."

"So you live here?" asked Maura.

"Absolutely!" replied the man.

"Pardon my frankness...but why? You've got nowhere to go, nothing to do...." I commented.

The man laughed. "I wouldn't put it that way exactly. I run the museum here."

"Sure, but, for who? The welcome to Shaniko sign says, 'Population 30.' "

"Aha! But that just means the people who live here. That doesn't include the campers, drive-bys like yourself, and the people that come in for Shaniko Days which, by the way, takes place later this week. You guys should drop in on your way back through."

"As great as you're making this sound, we've really gotta keep moving," said Maura.

"You're not hungry?" the man asked. " I thought growing teens were always hungry."

"I can't speak for her, but I'm starved!" I exclaimed.

"I could eat too," said Maura looking around, "But I don't see anything open."

"I'll make you a deal," said the man, "You take the museum tour and I'll give you each a sandwich for the road."

Maura mulled this over, pulling the cell phone out of her back pocket. "How long is this tour, and what's your full name in case you axe-murder us?"

The stranger's face lit with enthusiasm. "It won't take any longer than ten minutes. My name is George Edwards, current Museum Curator and Manager, and," he replied looking directly at Maura, "If I really wanted to axe-murder you, I'd have a long head start on whoever you're texting that info to."

Maura frowned, tucking her cell phone back into the pocket of her cut offs. "I'll take the gamble."

"I'll take the sandwich," I replied.

"And you will BOTH take the tour. Follow me!" called George, leading us across the street to the front porch of the

Shaniko Museum. Or what was left of it, really. It was hard to imagine the place was thriving business-wise.

"Shaniko," said George, "was originally called Cross Hollows. It was home to roughly 170 people but didn't really gain its place on the map until the railroad came through. Then we really became something. Did you know that Shaniko was once the wool capital of the world?"

"All due respect," said Maura, "until five minutes ago I didn't even know Shaniko existed."

"Well, little miss, we were a big deal for a bit there. You can never have too much information about the world you're living in."

Maura leaned over and whispered in my ear. "For the love of God, this better be one hell of a sandwich."

"For a good eight years there we were an "It" spot for farm and agriculture. Unfortunately, better railroad routes came into the picture and by 1942 the railroad stopped coming to Shaniko altogether. I could show you some things about wool and pioneer living, or I could show you the stuff the tourists really come for. Take your pick."

I shrugged. "Which gets us the better sandwich?"

"There is only one kind of sandwich, kid. Wool and pioneers or cars and wagons?"

"Cars and wagons it is!" hollered Maura.

"That's what I figured," sighed George. "No one ever comes for the wool." Sounding only slightly dejected, he launched into the next segment of a spiel I was beginning to get the impression he delivered a lot. "In the 1960s, people got real into historic preservation. In an effort to move with the times and keep people visiting Shaniko for more than a pit stop, the town filled the Sage Museum with classic cars and wagons. That part of the museum is closed today but I'm gonna let you in to look around anyway."

"How generous," exclaimed Maura.

"Generous, sure. You two might literally be the only humans I see today. Might as well make the tour interesting." The three of us entered the old car museum. There were several rows of vehicles all covered in a thick sheet of dust. The museum, like the town, had long since been abandoned.

"I thought you said you keep up the museum," I said.

'I do," replied George. "But the car and wagon portion is no longer being updated. Quite frankly, it has been closed to the public since 2014. We don't have money to add new cars and a museum with a stagnant exhibit isn't all that easy to sell admission to."

"Yeah but...this has got to be more appealing to the tourists than the wool stuff."

"You'd be surprised. Most of them are content to peer through the windows."

I ran my hand along the long smooth lines of an early 1900s Hupmobile. I wasn't a car junkie by any means, but Mom's second husband had been an absolute freak about classic auto shows. This place would have been his vision of paradise.

"The Hupmobile," said George, "is our oldest car. You probably recognize it from films like The Great Gatsby and Out of Africa. It was a big deal in its time. It used to draw a lot of attention here. Now I'm not so sure it even runs."

The rest of the cars were all Plymouth's, or what was left of them anyway. Most of the cars were more rust than paint at this point. The hood ornaments, commonly a status symbol on classic cars, were all mysteriously missing.

"There was a ton of theft there for awhile. Nowadays we don't worry about people sneaking in here. There isn't anything of value left to take besides the cars themselves, and you'd have to be an absolute magician to get a vehicle up running and out of here without my noticing. I tried to move one a few years back just for space purposes and it was a fruitless effort, to stay the least."

"So you just leave it this way now?" asked Maura.

"What else is there to do?" said George. "There's no money for restoration. What little we make on the museum goes back into the museum."

"I don't know," said Maura. "It just seems so sad. The idea that all of this is just rotting here when it used to be so beautiful."

"Are you a classic car fan?" asked George.

Maura smiled. "Hardly, but my father loves cars. He wanted to be a mechanic when he was a kid. He still kinda messes around with it. He'd really love this place."

"Bring him by then. It's not often I get a visitor with genuine interest."

A frown tugged at the corner of Maura's mouth. "I'd like to. I'll try to."

George seemed to read the situation well enough not to push for more details.

"That's about it kids. We've got cars, wool, wagons, and abandoned storefronts. Now, how about those sandwiches?"

My stomach growled in response.

"I'll take that as a 'yes,' then."

Instead of hitting the road, we opted to chow down with George at the picnic table in the park outside of the museum. Calling it a park was a bit of an exaggeration, given that it was really just a patch of grass with a picnic table and commemorative plaque. I had to hand it to George, though. He may have been a lackluster tour guide but he met the sandwich challenge with flying colors, especially when I told him I didn't eat meat and his original plan of turkey on rye was torpedoed on the spot. His substitution, however, was nothing short of awesome. The three of us worked our way through cream cheese, sprouts, farm fresh tomatoes, and cucumber on Dave's Killer Bread while George talked more about Shaniko and all the reasons we shouldn't miss the festival at the end of the week. We couldn't very well tell him why we were headed into the woods unattended without starting a conversation neither of us wanted to see to the end. So we lied, like terrible unappreciative teens with no respect for the kind of nice dudes who take time out of their day to make your road trip better. We said we'd be back, wouldn't miss it for the world. Shaniko Days would rock our world, etc., etc. But I could tell as we said our goodbyes that we weren't fooling George.

As we headed off toward Bend, I wondered how many other impromptu tours he'd given to pit-stop kids looking for snacks and a bathroom. Maybe I was being too much of a downer. It could work out, couldn't it? Maybe the return home would see us gloriously reunited, with Mike and his embarrassing caravan trailing behind us as we all stopped one last time in Shaniko for sandwiches and historical information we'd never use. I liked to think that was possible, but even Maura seemed to know we weren't headed for a happy ending.

Chapter Thirty: Maura

We stopped again when we got to Bend and picked up a map of the Cascade Lakes and copious amounts of Diet Coke to replenish the massive number of cans we'd both flown through on the drive. Our detour in Bend cost us 30 minutes of drive time. Dad wasn't kidding when he said the roundabouts would turn you around. One minute we were following the GPS as planned, and the next we were being rerouted...and rerouted...and rerouted yet again.

We were just about ready to give up and ask for help when we got our first hint we were headed in the right direction. There on the side of the road was exactly what we had been looking for: the sign for Cascade Lakes Recreation Area. Alex pulled the truck onto the shoulder as soon as it came into view. I'd never seen that rustic sign planted among the sagebrush and yet I knew it by heart. Dad may not have remembered the name of the lake, but he often spoke of the drive and how after you hit the sign, you better make sure you had a full tank of gas because the fun stuff wasn't for another 30 miles or so.

According to the sign, there were ten distinct recreation areas along the Cascade Lakes Scenic Byway. Three of the mile markers pointed toward reservoirs, a butte, and falls. Since we knew we were looking for a lake, we could narrow our search from ten to seven. Alex suggested that we follow the GPS to

Green Lake and camp there for the night. Whichever lakes we passed along the way could be eliminated from our search area. I really didn't want to stop and camp overnight, but the day had gotten away from us and every moment brought us closer and closer to nightfall. As badly as I wanted to start looking for Dad, I couldn't deny that Alex was right. We weren't going to find him the dark, nor would we find him by rushing through the process. We would camp tonight and start tomorrow fresh.

It was roughly 23 miles from the sign to the trailhead for Green Lake. But although Green Lake was allegedly a popular hiking destination, there were no signs marking it. Even with GPS we passed the turn twice. I was starting to lose my cool when Alex spotted a paper plate stapled to a telephone pole with "Green Lake Trailhead" scrawled in smeared ink. With not so much grace, he whipped the truck around, spewing gravel and dust in every direction.

"Sorry. It's been awhile since we ate. I'd like to get set up sooner than later, otherwise you're gonna meet the cranky version of me."

"As opposed to the delightful version of you I see so regularly?" Alex smiled,

"Precisely."

We parked at the trailhead and hiked the two miles up to the lake. The hiking reviews online had not been an exaggeration. The hike to Green Lake, though short, was beautiful. Most of the walk went through a valley created by two ancient lava flows. I tried to imagine my father taking this walk as a child. How different he must have been back then, when his body was a tool and not a prison. How hard would this walk have been for him now? Could he even get to the lake from the trailhead? I pushed the thought from my mind. I had to believe his time out here was worth it, otherwise it hurt far too much to know he was willing to leave us for it.

Although there were signs indicating severe punishment for camping in undesignated areas, we were running out of daylight. Given that we hadn't passed a single car on the way out here, we agreed it was worth the risk to set up camp as close to the lake as possible and pack up in the early morning before the rangers made their rounds. I hopped up into the truck bed and began tossing supplies out to Alex. The tent had to go up first. The rest could be done in the dark but it was always best to have a place to sleep. Our tent was the same one Nat and I used as kids, a small igloo for two, ideal for child assembly, which was apparently a good thing since judging by the look of things Alex had never assembled a tent in his life. With a certain amount of glee, I stood back to watch the struggle. There were poles shooting in each and every direction, the tent material pulling too tight across the top and too loose at the corners. Every 10 seconds or so, Alex would slap at a mosquito making dinner of his bare arms. Quite frankly, I could watch this forever. Alex wasn't a show-off by any means, but a part of me enjoyed knowing I was indisputably better than him at something. Even if it was a sad little skill like tent construction. After a steady five minutes of Alex wrestling with the tent, I quit pretending to arrange the rest of camp and lent him a hand. Before long we had the igloo up and stuffed with sleeping bags, pillows, spare clothes, and the food we didn't trust not to draw bears. I didn't know if bears even lived out here, but we were both from the "Hatchet" generation and unwilling to risk making any dumb, potentially life-threatening mistakes purely for the convenience of more tent space.

Once our tent was situated it was time to make a fire. I'd like to say we rubbed two sticks together Boy scout style, but that would be a dirty rotten lie. We followed Grandpa James explicit instructions for campfire assembly: "Assemble a teepee of firewood and douse that shit with lighter fluid." It wasn't a particularly woodsy smell but we had a fire in no time. I left the cooking up to Alex while I used the GPS and maps we picked up in Bend to plot out a course for tomorrow. Besides, whereas he might have been an invalid when it came to putting up a tent, I was an absolute disaster in the kitchen. I'd never survive in a world without a microwave.

Before long, Alex had rice and beans going on the camp stove with grilled zucchini wrapped in foil on the back end of the campfire. It would be a bit before dinner was ready, so I pulled two stumps up next to the fire and motioned for him to sit next to me. I spread the map across both our laps, trying not to blush from here to eternity when I felt his knees rest against mine.

"We passed Todd Lake on the way in and Sparks is only a mile from here. I could be wrong, but I doubt they would have stopped here after driving just one mile."

"Probably not."

"Same with Elk Lake. Dad always said they stopped at Green Lake because Uncle Andy begged to swim one last time before they headed back to Pendleton. My money's on either Lava Lake or Cultus Lake." I pointed to the two on the map.

"I thought you said the lake wasn't mapped."

"That's what Dad said, but that was in the early 70s. I looked some of these places up online last night, and even the smallest ones seem to have changed over the last few decades. This area is a lot more touristy than it used to be. Most of them are still primarily camping grounds, but a few have lodges now and small businesses where you can gas up your boat or rent gear for the water."

"Maybe someone at one of the lodges can identify the lake with the six-mile trail," Alex said.

I folded the map back up and neatly tucked it in the side of my Jansport backpack. For the daughter of an avid outdoorsman, I was a little late to the party when it came to having proper survival gear. My school pack was just about the only thing I could find to bring along. Alex wasn't much better off with his messenger bag slung over one shoulder and stuffed to the brim with snacks and extra underwear.

"So we start at Lava Lake?" I asked.

"Early as we can. Grandpa James wasn't messing around. If we aren't back in three days, we might as well not go back at all."

"That doesn't give us a ton of time," I groaned.

"It will have to do. We'll move smart and fast tomorrow. How big can these lakes really be anyway? Besides, you know what your Dad's stuff looks like and he's unlikely to camp too far from the water. Any further than a couple hundred feet into the trees and he'd be eaten alive by mosquitoes."

"Yeah, I guess. But if he doesn't particularly want to be found...."

Alex took my hand into his. "We'll find him Maura. I promise. One way or another, we'll bring your Dad back home."

Chapter Thirty-one: Alex

The closer it got to nightfall, the more paranoid I got about sharing a tent with Maura. "How paranoid?" you might ask. I casually suggested I sleep outside, actually used the phrase "under the stars," as if it was believable that I wanted to sleep outside in the cold, in maybe bear territory, just for the hell of it. There was no fooling Maura, though. She just laughed before informing me that we were both sleeping in the God-damn tent. If her snoring was a problem I could hike back down to the truck to sleep, but NO ONE was sleeping outside alone. How do you tell a girl, "I'm not afraid of your snoring, I'm just afraid of being a grown up?" This paranoia was all Grandpa's fault. If he had just neglected the safe sex chat altogether I wouldn't be here freaking out, thinking I'm about to lose my virginity to a girl I've known for three weeks and haven't even had the balls to kiss.

At this point I'd have done just about anything to avoid climbing into that tent, so I suggested we light the kerosene lamp and take a walk around the water's edge. It wasn't hard to figure out why Green Lake was called Green Lake. Even in the growing darkness, when you swung the light toward the water you could see the rich greens and turquoise that colored the surface. Some of it was the reflection from the volcanic mountains, but the rest was a mystery to me. It wasn't just the water that gave the Green Lake it's name. The grass and wildflowers that surrounded it were all a rich green, as was the thick layer of moss that crept its way from the grass to the waterline. From where we stood in the saddle of the valley, both the South Sister and Broken Top mountains reigned over the lake. The moon rose above Broken Top and lay its reflection across the water. It seemed the sky was filled with millions of stars, more than I'd ever seen in one place before. According to Maura, there were even more out there but the brighter the moon, the less you could see them. I wondered if I'd ever been anywhere more beautiful or if tonight was just the first time I stopped long enough to pay attention.

Beside me Maura took my hand in her own, leaning in close to lay her head on my shoulder. It occurred to me then that she might be my first real girlfriend. Everyone before seemed to pale in comparison. I'd never had a moment like this with another person. There were girls that I'd kissed, girls that I'd dated, girls that I'd kissed but never dated. But there was no one who made my stomach tie into knots the way it did when I was with Maura. I wanted to kiss her and I was terrified to kiss her all at once. It was as if I were afraid the spell would break and she'd be just another girl after that. I didn't want to give up the magic just yet.

We stayed that way for a long time, until the night air was too much and we couldn't stand without shivering from the cold. With the lamp in my right hand and Maura's in my left, we headed back to camp in silence. I liked the look of us, cast into long shadows by the moonlight on the forest floor. We were perfect in the dark, so perfect that I stopped being afraid about sharing a tent. I wanted to hold her, just hold her and I trusted myself to do that because I knew now unequivocally that I would do whatever it took not to ruin this.

Chapter Thirty-two: Maura

Alex waited outside the tent as I quickly changed from the day's shorts and graphic-T to sweats and a tank top. It would be cold in the tent but I likened full body pajamas to sleeping in a choke hold. I couldn't stand the way sleeves and necklines twisted around your body like a serpent in your bed. Besides, we could keep each other warm, right? I was ashamed to admit it, but at 17 years old I'd never actually cuddled before and I kind of wanted to. The way I saw it, there could never be a more perfect night or perfect person to cuddle with. With that in mind, I made a rash executive decision to zip our sleeping bags together. We would both be warmer this way, plus I was beginning to get the impression that any 'moves' made in this budding relationship were going to have to be made on my end. Not that I wanted to make big moves. Jesus Christ, I had the reputation for being a prude for a reason. All I really wanted was to feel close to another human being, in this situation a human being whom I happened to like a lot.

In the shadows cast from our lamp, I could tell that Alex had finished changing outside and was now hopping up and down to keep warm. It was now or never, I figured.

"All clear in here." I called.

Alex unzipped the tent, took one look at the new sleeping arrangements and began nervously popping his knuckles. "You switched things up a bit."

I hadn't actually expected him to say anything about the sleeping bags and was grateful for the darkness in the tent. Without it, I would have had to try and look calm and collected when, in reality, I was more than a little bit afraid he would insist we separate the bags and affirm my suspicion that even scantily clad and unsupervised, this boy wasn't attracted to me enough to take things to the next level.

" I figured it would be warmer this way."

"Uh huh."

If I looked nervous, Alex was petrified. He stayed rooted in place at the tent's front door, not an inch closer than when he had unzipped it. What if I was imagining the chemistry between us and he just wanted to be friends? When I really stopped to think about it, it was me who held his hand at the falls, me who put my head on his shoulder. I was suddenly filled with a tremendous self doubt. I decided to be as forward about NOT being forward as possible.

"I promise not to molest you in your sleep if that's what you're worried about."

Alex cracked a smile. "I'm a little worried."

"Come on. I'll keep my hands to myself unless instructed otherwise." I hopped into my side of the bed and flopped the covers down to make room for Alex. Alex took a deep breath before climbing inside, zipping up the tent, and blowing out the lamp. It was dark but I could feel the rustle of the sleeping bag as he crawled in beside me. For what felt like an eternity we lay flat on our backs, staring at the darkness in silence. When I thought I just about couldn't take it another second, Alex finally spoke.

"Maura?"

"Yeah."

"I haven't had sex before and I don't think I want to tonight."

I didn't know whether to be insulted or relieved. "I...um, haven't either. Did you think I had or that I wanted to?"

"No, yes, maybe? I guess I have no idea what I thought. I don't know much about you outside of these last three weeks. I mean, maybe you have boyfriends all the time, or maybe you're saving yourself for marriage. I didn't exactly want to just come out and ask you if you're a virgin right before heading out here unsupervised."

"What were you hoping I would say if you did ask?'

"Honestly? The very testosterone-filled boy part of my brain wanted you to say you'd done it before so I'd know I had a shot. The more realistic part of my brain hoped you'd say you were a virgin too because, quite frankly I'm scared shitless about having sex for the first time."

"So am I. And I don't think I'll be ready to anytime soon if that makes you feel any better."

Alex let out a nervous laugh. "It doesn't exactly make me feel better, Maura, but I'm kind of relieved."

"Considering we've only been seeing each other a few weeks, and by seeing each other I really just mean hanging out, what made you worried it had to be tonight?"

"A. hormones. B. Grandpa."

"Excuse me?!"

"I'm not even kidding. I let him get into my head. Last night he gave me a bunch of condoms and insisted I take them with me."

"Wow, your grandpa thinks a lot of me."

"Naw, it's not like that at all. You gotta think about it from his perspective. It's not like, an unusual thing for a 17-year-old boy to want to have sex. I mean it's pretty much expected. He just wanted to make sure I did the right thing, if we did, you know...do it. And he thinks a lot of you, Maura. He doesn't want me to screw up your life."

"I don't think you'd screw up my life by having sex with me." I didn't know why, but suddenly I was very defensive about when and who I got to have hypothetical sex with.

"So wait, you want to then?"

"No!" I cried.

"You don't? Because for a second you sounded like..."

"Alex! We're making this way too complicated. Like, I'm not even sure that other teens talk about this. I'm pretty sure they just do it and get it over with."

"I don't want to just get it over with."

"Neither do I. Sex is scary and permanent. I want to want to have sex without being afraid of it. Does that make sense?"

"More than you know," said Alex. "Can I just hold you then, without the groping and exchange of bodily fluids?"

I burst out laughing. "I'd like that very much!"

We spent the night cocooned together, his arms around my middle and his head resting in the crook of my neck. I listened carefully as his breathing slowed to a quiet rhythmic rest. I knew that at 17 I didn't have a clue what love was, but I was pretty sure it looked like this in the beginning.

Chapter Thirty-three: Alex

Neither Maura nor I needed the 6am alarm we had set the night before. We awoke the natural way, sunlight streaming through the tent, the call of birds cutting through the silence and reminding us all it was time to start the new day. I changed into my hiking gear, waterproof khaki shorts from REI, and a dark blue zip-up hoodie to stave off the cold till the morning sun had time to thaw the ground. Maura, on the other hand, was hell bent on freezing her ass off in the same pair of cut offs she'd worn yesterday and a lopsided sweatshirt she'd snagged from the stash of clothing her mother left behind. The sweatshirt was a murky gray color from years of wear, tear, and mothballs, but you could still make out the "Class of 79" logo peeling off the chest.

Maura showed me how to take down the tent and repack it without much fuss, and we were soon on our way back through the valley to the bottom of the trailhead where we'd left the truck. It was bittersweet, leaving the Green Lakes and beginning the search for Mike. Last night by the water's edge with the moon's reflection as our only company, it had been easy to forget why we were out here, easy to look at these three days in the mountains as some once-in-a-lifetime road trip with a girl I was falling for. But today was different. There was no longer time to meet quirky museum curators, stroll hand in hand, and just enjoy each other's company. Today we had a quest and it was either going to end well or it wasn't. For Maura, finding her father meant filling a hole in her heart, bringing something back home that never should have left in the first place. For me, bringing Mike back home meant keeping Maura and Natalie in the house next door. I was growing to love Grandpa James in a way that made it hard to picture ever going back to live with Mom and whatever good, bad, or terrible guy she was with at the moment. But if I were being truly honest, a lot of why I wanted to stay with Grandpa was Maura. It was my interest in her that opened the conversation channels between Grandpa and I in the first place. I couldn't bear the thought of those two as wards of the state, split into separate houses, grieving their father alone. It was as crucial to me as it was to those girls that we didn't leave these mountains without Mike.

It was a short drive between the Green Lakes and Lava Lake. Fortunately, it was far easier to find the turn for Lava than it had for Green Lakes. Just like the trailhead for Green Lakes, the turn off for Lava Lake was designated by a picnic plate stapled to a wooden pole. Apparently this was the not-so-official marking system for the Deschutes National Forest. Unlike the Green Lake Trailhead, campsites at Lava Lake were easily accessible and affordable enough that we didn't need to try and hide out from the rangers. We parked and paid for our spot before making our first round of the campsites. It was highly unlikely that Mike had swooped a legitimate campsite, but we weren't going to risk missing him over assumptions. Together, we looped the campsites down by the water. There was no sign of Mike's rig but that didn't mean he wasn't there. If his plan had been to avoid the crowds and camp out for 30 days, he wouldn't have been able to do it in a normal campsite, especially not here where there were only five official sites available.

No, if Mike were at Lava Lake, he would be further up the trail, much to my dismay, since mosquitoes seemed to find me wherever I went no matter how much toxic repellent I doused myself in. Maura, on the other hand, was one of those freakily blessed people who could be bitten by mosquitoes left and right and never have so much as a bump arise. While I slapped and swore profusely, she kept climbing as if nothing could faze her.

"How far on this trail are we willing to go?" I asked.

Maura stopped at the top of a gentle slope to pull out the trail map we'd picked up back at the campground. "If we stay on this trail for 4.7 miles, it connects with a section of the Green Lakes Trail. I vote we go that far and keep our eyes peeled for dirt bike routes. He may have taken a ranger road in, but once he arrived he'd have had to travel by bike to get around."

"If we don't see any signs of him there?"

"We can head back to camp for the night. Maybe someone will know about the 6-mile trail. It's just..." Maura frowned.

"It's just what?"

"There are a lot of trails on this map and there were tons on the brochure for Green Lakes, too. I don't think it's going to be as easy as asking which lake has a circular trail."

"No, probably not. But hey, Maura, what about the picture?"

"What about it?"

"Maybe someone around here would recognize the area."

"That picture was taken more than 20 years ago."

"Sure, but it's nature so how much can it really have changed?"

Maura paused to think it over. "Maybe."

"It's worth a shot."

"Only thing is, I didn't think to bring it with me."

"Not a problem. Look, if we get to where the two trails merge and we come up empty-handed, I'll call Grandpa and have him forward the picture. Do you think you could describe to Natalie where it's at?"

"That part's easy. I left it in our bedroom."

"Alright then! We have a Plan B. So...maybe, we can skip Plan A and get the hell out of this bug-infested wilderness?"

Maura laughed. "Not so fast, mosquito meat. He could still be out here. I'm not turning around until I know for certain that my father is not camping at this lake."

"Fair enough," I growled. "Lead on."

We continued up the Lava Lake trail for another two miles before Maura spotted an obviously man-made trail, fresh with the tire ruts from several dirt bike runs.

"Come on! This could be him. We have to follow it."

The trail wound up the mountain in the opposite direction of the path we had come. There was no guarantee it led to anywhere in particular, and a good chance we would lose our way trying to follow it.

"I don't know if we should take an unmarked trail. What if we can't find our way back?"

Maura rolled her eyes. We aren't going to find my dad on a marked trail, Alex, I thought that part was clear."

"I know, it's just, that's the complete opposite direction. Is it even on the map?"

Maura consulted the hiker's guide. "Look, we're here," she said, pointing to the midline of the Lava Lake Trail. "If we head in the direction of those ruts we'll eventually connect with here." She pointed to a summit near the edge of our map. "We can reconnect with the loop path below if we don't find him."

"That's, like, five miles in the opposite direction."

"And that's exactly where my Dad would want to be if he didn't want to be found. Are you with me or not?"

I was beginning to get frustrated and it was only noon. "Of course I'm with you. I wouldn't be out here if I wasn't with you. But you have to promise me that we head back to camp and call Grandpa by 4."

"Deal."

"And Maura, he might not be there. You shouldn't get your hopes up."

Maura smiled. "But he might be there, Alex. Get excited! This is our best and only lead thus far." She didn't wait for my response; within seconds she was bounding up the dirt road, filled with renewed enthusiasm. I had to remind her several times that I wasn't a runner and wasn't going to be able to keep up if she didn't slow the pace. I wanted to be excited for her, but I had a sinking feeling in the pit of my stomach that we weren't going to find more than a nice view at the top of this summit. I tried to imagine how I would feel if it were my own dad but I'd never had a dad and Mom wasn't half the parent Mike was to the girls. I wanted to find him and rub in his face what a good dad he was. Tell him to suck it up and look at his kids, they were perfect and he was responsible for that. They were smart, pretty, resilient girls who needed their father, but I knew it wasn't that simple. If seventeen years of raising Maura hadn't proved to him his merit on this earth, he wasn't going to suddenly see the light because a kid from Portland told him to get his shit together.

The longer the trail, the less and less confident I was that we would find Mike. He never could have gotten his truck this far and even if he had, we'd have come across it at some point. You couldn't exactly camouflage a huge Chevy with a flatbed trailer full of gas cans and water jugs. None of this seemed to faze Maura, who might have followed that trail to the end of the earth if it hadn't had a designated ending point.

We were a quarter mile from the summit when we heard voices coming through the trees. Maura stopped dead in her tracks, spun back on me with wide expecting eyes before yelling. "Let's go!" and sprinting up the trail.

In between my own gasps and pants, I could hear Maura screaming for her father the whole way up. What I didn't hear was a response. On my best day, I ran an eight-minute-mile, and that was on a flat track, not up a mountainside. Maura had me beat by at least a minute. By the time I reached the top, my heart was near explosion, my lungs gasping for air. I bent over to catch my breath, my hands perched on my knees the way they teach you to do in gym class. Only in gym class I never pushed myself to capacity.

From my hunched over position at the top of the hill, I scanned the landscape for Maura and the source of the voices we had heard below. They were both easy to find. Even with her face glued to her knees I could tell that the convulsing pile of tears perched on the stump fifty feet to my right was what was left of Maura's hope that we would find her father tonight. To her left was a band of bikers, if you could call them that. Did you call dirt bike riders "bikers" the way you did the tough Harley guys that hung outside of seedy bars? I wasn't sure and I wasn't sure I wanted to find out right now while we were a good five miles from the main trail and eight from camp.

I went over to Maura. I wanted to comfort her, but as far as boyfriendly duties went I was way out of my element. This whole trip was over and beyond your standard fare for a new relationship. What do you say to a girl who's bawling her eyes out over something you can't possibly comprehend? I wanted to say sorry and yet sorry didn't feel like half enough. It was moments like these that I wished I'd grown up in a normal family. Like, if I'd seen my Dad comfort my mother I'd know what to do. But it was never like that when I was a kid. If my mother was crying it was usually of her own doing. The closest

I'd seen to a normal functioning relationship was Grandpa and Grandma Jean, and that was just for a week at a time here and there, nothing I could count on.

It didn't take long for the bikers to take note of us. Next thing I knew the crew of four had formed a half circle around Maura and me. Up close they weren't so tough looking, mostly just dirty.

"Is she gonna be okay?" asked the tallest of the bunch. His face was covered in two days' worth of scruff, a futile attempt at hiding what was left of his baby face. Even so, it was clear that he and the rest of them were no more than 21. Not quite the rough and tough bikers I was worried about when I first saw them. In the back pocket of Baby Face, I could just make out the label on a flask of Jack Daniels. They were out here for a good time; crying girls were likely what they'd come out here to get away from, not engage with.

"I've got it under control," I replied. If they believed me, they were having a hard time showing it with their facial expressions.

"Is that right, miss? Everything all right?"

Maura straightened up when addressed directly. Using the sleeves of her sweatshirt to wipe the tears from her face, she responded barely above a whisper. "Everything's fine."

"If everything's fine, what's with the waterworks?" asked Baby Face.

"It's a long story."

"Maybe we can help?"

"I doubt it," scowled Maura.

"Try us."

Maura sighed. I could practically see the wheels turning in her head as she decided what she had to lose by filling these guys in.

I nudged her gently. "It can't hurt. Might as well explain."

"My father is missing," burst out Maura, " I came out here to find him and so far it's been just one dead end after another."

"Heavy," replied the biker, "How do you know he's out here?"

"I don't." said Maura. "It's a hunch. I saw your bike trails and I thought they might be his."

"Not too many people ride in the Deschutes forest. The trails are good, but they aren't well-known. Does he ride here often?"

"No. He hasn't been out here since he was a kid. He's not into riding. He just doesn't get around that well. He uses the bike more for transportation than fun."

"Bummer," said what appeared to be the youngest of the bunch.

"Have you tried the bigger lakes? There are trails all over the Deschutes. Lava Lake is good for a short ride, but there are tons of others he could be using to get around."

"We've still got a few to try. The problem is we're on a limited timeline. We have to be back home by tomorrow night."

"Yikes, you've got a lot of ground to cover for 24 hours. I don't mean to be a downer, but you're not gonna find him if you go chasing every bike trail you come across."

"Trust me, I'm beginning to get that impression." said Maura.

"What information have you got to work with?"

"Not much," mumbled Maura.

"Actually," I piped up, "We've got a picture! It's old, but we think he might have tried to go to the place in the picture."

"Now you're talking!" hollered the biker, his face beaming with pride. " No one knows the Deschutes better than us. Show us the picture and I bet we can identify the area!"

"Seriously?" cried Maura.

"Absolutely," smiled the leader. "I'm Nick, by the way, and this is Luke, Aiden, and Tom."

I put my hand out for a shake. "I'm Alex and this is Maura."

"Pleasure to meet you. Have you got that picture on you?"

Maura grimaced, "Not yet. But we can get it just as soon as we get back to camp where I can get a cell signal."

Nick consulted with the group. "What do you say, guys? Give the kids a lift back to camp?"

Maura's face lit with renewed hope.

"Have you ever ridden a dirt bike before?" asked Luke.

Maura grinned. "Ridden no, driven yes."

"My kind of girl," said Luke. "She's with me. One of you others can play human backpack with him."

Nick rolled his eyes. "Alright then, you can ride with me. Just give us a second to get packed up. We have a rule up here: Whatever you bring in, you pack out, no exceptions."

After a few minutes of scouring the forest floor for cigarette buds and other signs of destruction, the six of us loaded up the bikes. I'd never ridden or driven a dirt bike before but any fear I had was wiped away by the sight of Maura's smile, wide and gleaming, as she flew down the mountain.

Chapter Thirty-four: Maura

Refreshed from the ride back, I offered to make dinner for the crew in exchange for their help finding Dad. While I prepared the night's meal of grilled Polish dogs and one nasty-looking tofu creation for Alex, Alex called home and arranged for Natalie to text the picture of Dad and Grandma at the lake. For an eight-year-old, Nat was kind of a tech wizard. In less than ten minutes, Nick and the rest of the bikers were poring over the picture. They were also pouring an awful lot of whiskey and beer, which made me far less confident in their ability to recognize the background of a photo from two decades ago.

Luke and Nick (clearly the leaders of this four-man crew of hooligans) were the first to show any recognition. Only problem was, they didn't quite agree on which lake the picture was taken at. Luke was positive they were at Cultus Lake and Nick was just as positive that they were looking at Little Cultus, the red-headed stepchild of the now apparently very popular weekender's hot spot. Big Cultus had a resort and a trail that both circled the lake and traversed up to a summit at the top of Cultus Mountain. It could be the trail my Dad talked about, but there was no easy way to tell. According to Nick, who'd grown up riding the trails of the Deschutes Forest, Cultus Lake had had a handful of new owners over the last 20 years and, along with new ownership, came the development of new hiking paths and campsites. The original six-mile trail might still exist, but it was likely connected to a half dozen others by now. Just when I was starting to get discouraged, Luke had a lightbulb moment.

"You said your Dad was staying long term, right?"

"Thirty days is what he told us, but he also lied and said he was hunting in the Blue Mountains, so..."

"Yeah, yeah, I get it. Your Dad's being a bit of a shit but that's not my point. If he was staying long term then he must have brought quite a bit of supplies along with him, yeah?"

"Loads. He brought extra gas for the bikes, and enough clean drinking water to get him through a sizeable chunk of time. Plus, you know, his bow for hunting, clothing, tent, the whole nine yards."

"So a truck and trailer?"

"Yes."

"Excellent!" cried Luke.

I hadn't quite caught onto Luke's enthusiasm. "What about that is good news?" I asked.

"Look," he said. "If your Dad is at either of the Cultuses, we'll know which one. You can't get across the lake to the real camping area with a vehicle. The only route over is by boat, hike, or bike."

"Which means?" asked Alex.

"Which means we find the parking lot with your Dad's truck in it and we find the lake he's hiding out at."

I was so unexpectedly happy I could have exploded. How had we not thought of this already? Without thinking I flung my arms around Luke's neck.

"Thank you, thank you, thank you!" I cried, burrowing my face in his left shoulder.

Luke, apparently not used to overzealous demonstrations of female affection, pulled away quickly. "You're welcome," he mumbled. "We'll ride with you over to the Cultuses in the morning. If we find your Dad's truck, we can give you a lift across the lake. After that, I'm afraid you'll be on your own, seeing as how we aren't exactly welcome on the trails over there."

"Aren't welcome?" inquired Alex.

"Let's just put it this way," said Nick. "We haven't always been as diligent with that whole 'pack it in pack it out' bit. The rangers over there aren't huge fans and I'd just as soon avoid any unnecessary contact."

"Deal!" I cried. "And," extending my arms to showcase the slew of food I'd laid out on our campsite picnic table, "your extremely classy dinner buffet awaits." I watched in wonder as the five boys loaded their plates with Polish dogs, heaping mounds of Ruffles, and enormous scoops of my homemade potato salad. By the time they were finished filling their plates, there was one lone dog and a poor man's serving of potato salad left for me to dig into. Ordinarily I could go toe to toe with any man's appetite, but not tonight. Tonight I was too excited to eat much anyway. Alex and I sat knee to knee on the log we'd managed to drag over as seating for the fire, watching incredulously as the four boys polished off their dinners in a matter of minutes. It was like they hadn't eaten in days. Drinking, however, it appeared they'd been doing a lot of lately. I'd long since lost count of how many beers they'd pulled out of the cooler since arriving back at camp. The more they drank, the louder they got, and the more worried I became that their trouble with the rangers was going to carry over to Lava Lake as well. They had to tone it down before the other campers went to bed for the night.

Fortunately, I didn't have to worry for long. When the darkness began to descend on the lake, Aiden - the youngest, quietest of the bunch - made a suggestion the rest couldn't refuse. "Night fishing?" he inquired.

The other four exchanged a gleeful look amongst themselves. "Night fishing!" they yelled in unison, clinking what was left of their four cans together in a drunken circle of joy.

"And you two are coming with," ordered Nick. "You can't spend three nights in the Cascade Lakes and NOT go night fishing."

I looked to Alex, unsure what his reaction to such an invitation would be. The longer I spent with him, the more aware I became that this trip was not part of normal teenage dating. Most kids had months to get to know each other before they had to make tough decisions like whether or not to get in a stranger's boat at 9pm. I knew the softball stuff about Alex. What kinds of food he liked, how he liked to cut his hair, and just how short you could wear your shorts without him having trouble looking away. I didn't know how he responded to peer pressure. Apparently with a rather large grin.

"What are we waiting for?" asked Alex. "Let's go catch breakfast!"

Nick burst out laughing, his cheeks flushed in the lamplight. "The first thing you should know about night fishing is you never catch any fish."

"And the second?" asked Alex.

"If at first you don't succeed, try until the first guy passes out."

"Grrrreat," I grumbled. "Sounds super safe."

Alex slung his arm around my waist, pulling me in close. "I'll protect you from the big bad drunks. I'm well seasoned in the art of putting drunks to bed. Besides," he whispered, his lips so close to my ear I could feel his breath, "After they pass out, it's just you and me on a boat in the moonlight. I can't pass that up."

I felt the warmth rising in my cheeks and other places too. Now it was me whose ability to withstand peer pressure I doubted.

Chapter Thirty-five: Alex

I'd never been on a boat like this before. In sixth grade, I'd gone to outdoor school where they made you canoe in groups of four. I'd gone white water rafting my first year of high school, and when I was really little Grandpa took me out on a fishing boat. But I'd hardly consider Grandpa's little aluminum skiff in the same category as the beast before me. Luke's boat, or his father's to be precise, was built for speed, not fishing. According to Luke, the 26-foot cherry red hull could comfortably carry eleven and not so comfortably carry up to sixteen - if that is, you didn't mind riding a little closer to the water. I did mind. It wasn't like I was afraid of going fast, I just didn't particularly want my maiden voyage to be my last voyage. Fortunately, it was just the six of us and Luke promised to be a 'gentle, responsible driver.' Kinda hard to believe considering how many beers he'd already been through, but I was in no condition to negotiate.

By the time we had a cooler full of beer and soda iced and loaded on the dock, darkness had already begun to descend on the lake. Maura, who'd apparently spent a great deal of her childhood on and off of speed boats, made herself useful scurrying along the side of the boat, disconnecting the blue foam buoys that kept the vehicle from slamming into the dock at each passing wave. I watched as she carefully untied the ropes from each cleat, stashing the ties and bouys in the built-in panels that flanked each side. With Maura at the bow and Luke at the rear right, the two pressed gently against the dock, allowing us to drift quietly into the deep. Once we were clear of the dock entirely, Luke took his seat behind the wheel with Maura kneeling on the back of the seat behind him.

Nick and I sat in the back, one on either side of the motor, the cooler propped between us for safekeeping. With the boat steadily drifting toward the center of the lake, Luke lowered the motor, its rudders swiveling in slow succession as it carved into the smooth water. We were the only boat off the dock. Each sound we made carried back to shore as if we were standing at the bottom of the Grand Canyon shouting up.

"Hold on in the bow," Luke called to Tom and Aiden. The two grabbed the railing, smiles plastered across their faces. I leaned over to ask Nick if it was really necessary to hold on, but before I could get the words out the kick of the engine thrust me backward. My stomach plummeted, the adrenaline shooting through my body the way it does those first 10 seconds on the slope of a roller coaster. The once silent lake was now filled with the buzz of our engine cutting through the water at rapid speed. Up front, Tom and Aiden braced the railings as the bow gradually lowered into the water, descending from launch mode to a steady plane. I looked back at the wake behind us, amazed that one boat could cause so many waves.

"It's great for wakeboarding!" yelled Nick, his voice barely carrying over the rush of the wind.

"I've never been," I called back.

"You're crazy!" he yelled. "What's the point of growing up in Oregon if you've never ridden a dirt bike or wake boarded?"

I didn't have an answer. I knew what my old friends would say. Heck, I knew what I would have said a month ago: Dirt biking and watersports? Not for me. Give me Me First and the Gimmie Gimmies at the Wonder Ballroom, waffle carts after midnight, girls who wore glitter on their eyelids, movie theatres that served beer, and pizza in Lazyboys. That was the point of growing up in Oregon, or so I used to think. Now, well, now I didn't know what to think. I still loved those things, still missed those things, but right now, with my body pressed into the seat behind me, night air coursing through my veins and the most incredible girl I'd ever met five feet away from me, looking like the cover of a Nicholas Sparks movie, I wouldn't have traded this moment for any of those things.

The boat slowed to a stop in the middle of the lake.

"Here's as good a place as any," said Luke, turning off the ignition. He knelt down between the driver's side seat and the passengers to pull up the false floor where he stored extra life jackets, fishing poles, and an ancient anchor. Maura hopped down to help, grabbing extra rope from a side compartment and tying a sailor's knot around the anchor. With one solid heft, she tossed the anchor over the side of the boat. One moment it was a loud splash, the next dead silence as it drifted down below the dark surface. Beside me, Nick popped open the cooler.

"Coors or Pabst?" he asked.

"Neither," I replied.

Nick raised one eyebrow. "You're not about to tell us you only drink IPA are you? Because that would seriously lower my opinion of you."

"Naw, I just don't drink."

"A goody-goody eh?"

"No, more like a self preservation thing. My family doesn't exactly do well with the bottle. One's never enough, that sorta thing."

Nick nodded, popping open his own can. From across the boat I caught Maura's eye. We never talked about it, the things that were wrong with our families. Kinda like how we never talked about why Mike left them or why neither of our mothers were around. She knew as well as I did that Grandpa James spent more time in the bottle than out, but aside from a lighthearted joke at his expense here and there we avoided those hard conversations. It wasn't like I was afraid of opening up to her. I've always been a fairly good communicator. The thing was, Maura was not so great when it came to the tough stuff. She tended to avoid the difficult talk until forced to deal. I didn't remember much about Mike from my childhood visits, but I got the impression it was an inherited trait.

"What about you, Maura?" asked Nick. "Can I toss you a beverage?"

"I'll take a Diet Coke," she responded, winking in my direction.

"Suit yourselves," said Nick. "More for the four of us."

"That's what I'm counting on," said Maura.

"And why is that? inquired Luke.

"Because," said Maura, "The sooner you pass out, the sooner I get to drive the boat."

"Drive the boat!" hollered Luke, "That, my dear, is wishful thinking. No one drives the Jagged Little Pill but me."

Both Maura and I burst into laughter. "Tell me you're kidding? Your boat is not named after an Alanis Morissette song," said Maura.

"Take a peek over the side," called Aiden from the bow. Sure enough, there it was: Jagged Little Pill, scrawled in large silver lettering across the port side.

"Lets just say my dad's midlife crisis happened at the same time as that album's heyday." said Luke. "At the time, we thought it was pretty cool. The whole family voted on it, actually."

"I'm afraid to hear what the other nominees were," said Maura.

"Ah," replied Luke. "I'm glad you asked. It was between Rosie Rosie - which is, incidentally, also what my sister Aly wanted to name our youngest sibling - and Dream Catcher."

"And how did you make the ultimate decision?" I inquired.

"That part was easy. We all vetoed Rosie Rosie on account of it's never a good idea to let your five-year-old name a $30,000 piece of equipment, and Dream Catcher got the boot after my oldest sister's family history report revealed we were a lot less Native American than my dad thought."

"Grandma wasn't a Cherokee princess after all, eh?"

"Exactly. Besides," said Luke. "We've all come to love Jagged Little Pill, corny name and all."

With the anchor down and the night beginning to wane, the four of them baited and cast their lines. I didn't know much about boats, but I knew my way around a speaker system and the one built into Jagged Little Pill was nothing to shrug at. Because the boat was designed for water sports, wakeboarding in particular, it had the kind of speakers that attached to your wake tower and cast a sound so full you could hear it with the wind whipping in your face while being dragged at fifty miles an hour behind the boat. With Luke's permission, I connected my iPhone to the auxiliary. There was one condition.

"Only country," proclaimed Luke.

"Only country on a boat named after a pop song?"

"Driver decides!" said Luke.

With no desire to argue with our new, ultra helpful friends, I opted to compromise by throwing on a combination of typical Pendleton country fair; Gary Allen; Garth Brooks; terrible, terrible Brad Paisley; and a few of my favorite alt country songs by the Old 97's. I wouldn't go so far as to say it was my intention to put the guys to sleep, but I certainly wasn't disappointed when the last of the four nodded off around midnight. I might not know much about dirt biking or even the great outdoors, but I knew alcohol, and there was no way those boys were going to make it past midnight after a full day of drinking in the sun at high elevation.

It was just the two of us now. Aiden and Tom had moved to the back hours ago for better "fishing," aka access to the cooler, and Luke and Nick were passed out with the seats extended in the middle of the rig. Maura and I sat in the bow, me with my legs on either side of her, her leaning back against my chest. From the center of the lake, there were no lights to interrupt the stars, nothing but the music and the stillness of the water.

"Hey Maura?" I whispered.

"Hmm?"

"What happens after tomorrow?"

"What do you mean?"

"I mean when we go back. When the summer's over. What then?"

"I hadn't really thought about it," she replied. "You leave, I suppose. You leave, Grandpa James starts drinking again, Nat will miss you like crazy. No one has ever been willing to spend time with her like that before."

"Just Nat, huh?"

"And me." Maura spun around to look at me, "Alex, I'm gonna miss you like crazy. You know that, right?"

I tightened my grip around her waist. "I hoped so. I hoped that a lot, actually." In the moonlight, I could just make out the glisten in the corner of her eyes.

"Let's not talk about it now, okay? Tonight can just be tonight, with no thoughts about tomorrow."

"Deal," I whispered. "I've got an idea."

"Yeah?"

"Yeah," I said, hopping up and stepping around Luke to where my iPhone sat connected to the sound system.

"Only country," mumbled Luke mid snore.

I stood still for a moment to be sure he was still asleep before opening my favorite playlist. With a smile, I hit play on Ed Sheeran's "Hearts Don't Break Around Here."

"You're breaking the rules," whispered Maura.

"It'll be worth it," I promised, stepping across the seating and over the railing to the long smooth plastic of the bow.

"What are you doing?" asked Maura skeptically.

"Trust me," I called softly, reaching my hand down to pull her up with me. "Will you dance with me, Maura?"

Hesitantly, she took my hand. "I'm not that great at this." she warned.

"You can't mess this up," I whispered, pulling her close.

Together we swayed with the rhythm of the boat, her head on my shoulder, my lips in her hair. We danced long into the night, till the playlist faded out and the stars gave way to the sunrise. She was, in that moment, everything I wanted for myself. It was becoming abundantly clear to me that losing her was not an option. When I got home, I'd call Mom and tell her I wasn't coming back to Portland, or anywhere else she and Husband Number Four had in mind. Maybe, if I was feeling brave, I'd even tell her that I wasn't going to manipulate Grandpa for her, either. Maybe, I'd tell her to grow up for once. It was easy to think courageous thoughts right now with a beautiful girl - the beautiful girl really - leaning into my chest making me believe I was finally worth something.

As the morning sun rose over the lake, Maura drove the boat back towards camp. If Luke objected, he wasn't doing a great job of complaining. Nick and he were practically spooning in the passenger side seat, oblivious to the steady rock of the boat as Maura cruised cooly across the quiet lake. It was still early, but we were no longer the only boat on the water. All around us slalom skiers cut through the water, weaving back and forth across the wake with a grace and balance I'd never seen in person before. Maura was a masterful driver, managing to direct the boat away from the skiers without disrupting their course or creating waves. When a skier bit it and hit the water unexpectedly, she would quickly redirect, sometimes before even the driver noticed the fall. By the time their orange flag was up and flying, Maura would already be headed safely away. I wasn't that good at driving a car, and there were roads and rules for all of that.

"Where'd you learn to do this?" I asked.

Maura smiled.

"When my Mom was around the four of us camped a lot. We all used to, actually. Grandpa, Uncle Andy, the cousins, everyone. My dad had these rules. You learn to swim without a life jacket, you get to stay up around the campfire with the grown ups. Learn to ski and you get to go out to pick up the crawdad traps. Don't ask me why that was appealing but it was.

Last and best, if you learned to ski on one ski, he'd teach you to drive the boat."

"You can ski on one ski?" I asked incredulously.

"Well," laughed Maura. "Not really, but the summer I turned ten I managed to stay up for a whole twenty seconds. He honored his end of the deal."

"Your dad sounds pretty great," I said.

"Yeah well, that was a long time ago," said Maura. With precision she slowly pulled the boat up to the dock, shutting off the engine once we were close enough to tie off.

"Should we wake them?" she asked, motioning toward the four sleeping boys.

"Naw," I replied, tossing her a couple of towels from the under carriage. "The sun will wake them soon enough. Better to let them sleep it off. You and I should get an hour or two of sleep in anyway."

Maura yawned.

"I suppose you're right. Not too long though, okay?"

I nodded in agreement. Together, we covered the boys the best we could with the towels and headed back to our campsite where our tent was waiting. Never before had a sleeping bag on a bed of pine needles looked so appealing. Together we crawled into bed, too tired to change into pajamas, too tired for conversation. I wrapped my arms around her, nuzzling my head in the crook of her neck. We both knew that when we woke our world would be infinitely more complicated, but right now the exhaustion of a day spent searching and a night spent dreaming left us too exhausted to pretend we weren't still children.

Chapter Thirty-six: Maura

I awoke with a start. The day that stretched ahead of me held far more fear than comfort. I didn't know what was worse: Finding my father or coming no closer to him than before we had left Pendleton. He'd been gone for 21 days without once checking in. How long had it been since he'd given up? Was it before his trailer left the drive? Before his last hug to Natalie? Or did things change once he got out here? What if I didn't ever get to know? What if when we left this afternoon it was to return home to Natalie and tell her it was just the two of us now? I didn't know if I could do that. I didn't know if I could be the things that Natalie needed, and worst of all I had a bad feeling I didn't *want* to be. Beside me Alex was still snoring peacefully. I hated to wake him but I couldn't lay still any longer. I needed answers. I needed a strategy for the future. I needed to yell at my father till the sound of my own voice was too much for even me to take.

I nudged Alex awake and unzipped the tent, the early morning sunlight flooded through the door flap, far too bright for anyone to sleep through. I worried it would take some doing to get Alex up and moving, but the call of nature was apparently strong enough to motivate even the tiredest of teenage boys. Much to my surprise, Alex and I were not the first awake. In the camp next door, the smell of strong camp coffee made itself known. The boys had already taken down their tents, loaded their bikes and boat onto the trailer behind Luke's enormous truck, and were now hovering around the fire while Aiden prepared a breakfast of thick cut bacon and scrambled eggs. Luke hollered at us from across camp.

"It's about time you two rolled out of bed. Breakfast is in ten minutes. Get your truck packed and we'll head out before it starts to get hot." Alex and I didn't waste any time. It had been hours since my last meager meal and I was starving. The six of us ate in silence, the weight of the day resting heavily upon all of us. When it was time to head out, Luke suggested we follow him since he knew his way in and out of the campgrounds as well as all of the places along the way you could park a truck and trailer without getting ticketed. Alex and I didn't argue. Back in the truck as we wound our way up Cascade Lakes Highway, Alex did his best to make conversation.

"I talked to Grandpa James this morning. I let him know we won't be home till tonight but that we're on the right track."

Nervously I bit at the sides of my cuticles. "Did he agree to that?"

Alex shrugged. "He wasn't happy but he promised not to call CPS so long as we check in throughout the day."

I sighed with relief. "You're lucky. He's a good guy."

"Yeah," agreed Alex. "But he hides it well, doesn't he?" The two of us laughed, somewhat breaking the tension.

"He uh, said Natalie's doing well too. She got her splint off and Elizabeth brought her sister over yesterday so she's not dying of boredom over there."

"God, I feel shitty for not even asking."

"You've got a lot on your mind," Said Alex, giving my knee a gentle pat, a pat that turned into a rub, that somehow became a permanent hand placement on my leg.

"Getting a little comfortable there, eh?" I smirked.

"Oh, you may have missed the memo. We're a thing now. Which means I get to make moves now until you swat me away. I'll be trying with frequency and dedication so you should probably prepare yourself defensively." I laughed.

"Oh, is that how it works?"

"Yes, standard teenage boy practice."

"I see. And what new perks do I get?"

Alex mulled this over, pretending to scratch the non-existent beard on his chin. "You get to demand inconvenient things like purse carrying and homecoming dance attendance."

I smiled at the idea of walking through Pendleton High School hand-in-hand with Alex. I was no longer afraid of my reputation as a prude, seeing as how Alex was secretly a touch on the shy side himself.

"So you're serious about staying in Pendleton, then? You're really gonna move in with Grandpa James, like, permanently?"

"It's still up to my Mom, but despite her rather consistent selfish streak she's still a good Mom deep down. She'll want me to be happy and Grandpa James isn't getting any younger. There aren't a ton of great options. Only three really. Either I move in with him, she moves in with him, or Aunt Renata does and there is no way she is letting Aunt Renata weasel her way into Grandpa's life now that he's actually old enough to start drafting a will."

"And you don't think she'll be wanting to relocate to Pendleton?"

"Ha!" barked Alex. "My mother wouldn't move back to Pendleton for all the money in the world."

"She sounds like my mother."

"The two of them would get along I'm sure. The only difference is my mom waited till she left Pendleton to get pregnant with me."

"Wise choice," I grumbled.

"I don't know," said Alex "I'm glad you were born here. I wish I'd known you longer."

Alex was the only person in the world who could make me smile on a day like today. I planned right then and there to keep him.

"Oh, heads up!" I called. "Luke's turning left up ahead." Following close behind we pulled the truck in, taking the long winding dirt road that circled Big Cultus. From the passenger side window, I could just make out the dark blue of the lake through the pine trees dotting the shore. We drove for about a mile, passing what Luke called the "yuppy campsites." Yuppy campsites, he warned us, were the ones that line a paved road and had direct access to running water and clean outhouses. It's not where the locals stay when they come here. It's for the families who throw their kids in a tent to keep them occupied, but can't be bothered to exit their fifth wheel when it rains. It was obviously not where we would find my father. Once we had passed family camping, we reached the main parking lot and boat dock. According to the signs, Dad could park his truck for up to 14 days at a time before anyone would bother interrupting him.

"I think it would be smarter to park and walk through than try and spot the truck while driving," suggested Alex. I agreed. Besides it was Friday afternoon and the weekend campers were all clamoring to get parked and across the lake before the good lakeside sites filled up. The last thing we wanted was to be stuck in a never ending circle of boat trailers looking for a place to park. Luke and the boys followed our lead, pulling over to the side of the road and hopping out to inspect the parking lot.

"We're gonna head into the Lodge and grab a drink," said Luke. "If you find what you're looking for, come grab us and we'll see what we can do about getting the boat into the water. I should have warned you it would be busy today. August is really the last good time to camp at Big Cultus so there will be a lot of regulars in and out today."

"Regulars?" I asked.

"Yeah, people who come every year. It's a beautiful place and you can't beat the ski course. We used to be regulars when I was a kid."

"Not anymore, eh?" remarked Alex.

"Yeah well, like I said before. I did some boneheaded things last year after Dad died."

"Oh," I mumbled "I didn't realize…."

"It's cool," said Luke changing the subject. "You didn't really think any responsible father would let his 20-year-old son take a boat and truck this nice out for recreation, did you? Yeah, not so much. I inherited it. Silver lining, that sort of shit."

"I see."

"Anyways," interrupted Aiden. "They make a killer Oreo Shake at the Lodge. Come grab us if you find what you're looking for."

"Will do," said Alex.

The two of us watched as the boys headed up past the boat ramp to the trail that led from the parking area to the great red lodge on the hill. If we had been here for any other reason, I'd have loved to go with them. From a distance, the place reminded me of Kellerman's from Dirty Dancing. We circled the parking lot, beginning close to the water where small cars and trailers fit for wave runners occupied most of the spaces. Continuing past we began to see more SUVs and other family vehicles, none occupying spaces large enough to hold a trailer and thus none that could have fit my dad's set up. I was beginning to lose confidence when we reached our first truck and trailer combo. The rest of the parking lot, though quite a distance from the boat ramp, was better fit for bigger vehicles. It was where Luke would park if he were camping tonight and where my Dad would be if he was here. I told myself not to hold my breath. That we would walk through as many times as it took. That we would look carefully at each vehicle and make sure we didn't miss Dad's, that we had time now thanks to Alex's call back home. I told myself all of this, but none of it mattered because there at the end of the parking lot sat the unmistakable winking eyes of my dad's homemade flatbed.

Chapter Thirty-seven: Alex

I was starting to get used to chasing Maura. Not so used to it that I wasn't out of breath, but used to it enough that I understood when to kick it in high gear and chase the girl. This was one of those times. At the end of the lot, in all its ghetto, redneck glory sat Mike's pick-up. Maura wasn't kidding when she said Natalie had done a number on the back gate. Even across the dusty parking lot there was no mistaking that pink monstrosity. By the time I caught up with Maura, she had already jimmied the front lock.

"What exactly are you looking for?" I asked.

"Signs of life!" replied Maura. "Proof that he's been here recently."

What we found was not uplifting. Though the remains of a Burgerville lunch lay crumbled in its brown paper bag, the receipt was dated the very day Mike left. Now, it was possible that Mike was lousy at throwing out his trash; hell, there were still empty wrappers littering Grandpa's truck from our stop in Bend two days ago. But the longer we looked around, the more it became evident that Mike hadn't been back to this truck in quite some time.

"Hey!" came a voice from behind us. "This rig belong to you?" Maura and I crawled out of the cab to see the speaker. Before us stood a Deschutes forest ranger, fully decked out in his dark brown UPS-style uniform. "Ranger Armstrong" was embroidered in gold thread across his right breast pocket in case there was any question who we were dealing with.

"It belongs to my Dad," said Maura. "We're looking for him. Have you seen anyone? Coming in and out of this truck?" It was a long shot, but still worth asking.

Ranger Armstrong shook his head pointing to Mike's windshield. "You see those yellow slips of paper under the wipers? Those are tickets. You can't park here for longer than fourteen days. This rig's been here over a week past the maximum stay. Unless he's coming across the lake to get in at night, this thing hasn't been touched in at least a week. Realistically, longer."

Maura nodded, the hope she'd felt just moments before slowly morphing back into doubt.

"When you kids find him," said the Ranger. "You let him know he has to move his rig, tonight, not tomorrow, not the next day. There are plenty of people coming up for the weekend who need a place to park."

"Pardon me mister," snapped Maura. "When and IF I find my father, his parking tickets are going to be the last thing on my mind."

Ranger Armstrong tipped his hat at Maura. "My apologies, miss." He reached into his breast pocket to retrieve a card. "If you need any sort of assistance, give the station a call. Cell reception sucks across the lake but if you head out to the end of the dock, you'll be able to place a call."

Begrudgingly Maura accepted his card before stomping off toward the lodge. I was all set to apologize to the Ranger but he was already making his rounds, checking the dates on each vehicle's permits, ticketing those who had been there too long or hadn't bothered to pay at all.

This time I opted not to chase Maura. I got the distinct feeling there would be plenty more running once we hit the other side of the lake. It was a short but leisurely walk up to the Cultus Lake Resort and Lodge. "Resort" was a pretty fancy term for what I was looking at. There was no hotel, just cabins along the tree line. The cabins were painted a dark, barn red with deep green trim to match the main building. There was a man-made beach at the base of the Lodge, complete with both a beach and water volleyball set up. You could rent stand-up paddle boards, kayaks, paddle boats, you name it, but most of the equipment sat untouched. The families there were content to play in the sand or paddle around in the shallow waves that slowly drifted over from the boat launch. A long rock staircase wound up through the trees from the shoreline to the outdoor deck of the main lodge. There were lounge chairs everywhere painted a crisp white to complement the numerous pots of brightly-colored flowers. The chairs, like the rental equipment below, were mostly vacant. If the lodge was doing well business-wise, it did a hell of a job hiding it.

By the time I entered the restaurant portion of the Lodge, Maura, Luke, and the rest of the gang were already at the front counter closing out the tab on Aiden's milkshake. Luke was purchasing what appeared to be a hideous ball cap with "Cultus Lake Fishing" scrawled over a hideously embroidered depiction of what was meant to be a bass. The six of us headed back down the path toward the boat ramp.

"I didn't exactly take you for the souvenir type," I said, motioning toward the hat.

"Not for me," said Luke, grabbing Maura by the wrist. Carefully he shoved the hat over her head, remembering to pull her ponytail through the back slot. "The elevation is pretty high here. You're gonna burn whether you wear lotion or not. That beanie will keep you covered," he said, motioning toward me. "but she's gonna fry her scalp if you have to do any real climbing."

"Thanks," said Maura. "I hadn't thought about that."

"Hazards of having sisters," said Luke.

It was a long process getting Luke's Dad's giant truck in the right position to back the boat into the water. Luckily, the four of them had done it enough times that Maura's and my only real job was to stay out of the way. Together, we stood on the rock peninsula that connected with the ramp dock and watched as family after family brought their gear from the parking lot to the boat ramp. Some had so much stuff you'd think they were moving there for good, while others, clearly day campers, brought just the essentials, like coolers, life jackets, skis, and inner tubes. It was easily 85 degrees out, and how I longed to be a camper, out here for fun, nothing to worry about but whether or not it would look bad that I was somewhat terrified of water sports.

Once Jagged Little Pill was safely secured to the dock and Nick had taken the truck back to park for the afternoon, we were free to load up for the trip across the lake. Here in the mid morning air as we cruised across the lake at tremendous speed, I was no longer nervous about the ride. In fact, I found myself sitting up front, leaning over the bow like Leonardo Dicaprio in the Titanic. It really did feel like flying, the wind tearing through you, the feeling that gravity didn't exist, and nothing could touch you. I wanted more trips like this. Minus the rescue mission. I made a mental note to get the guys' contact information before we split. Maybe we could come back next summer and the summer after that, become regulars like Luke talked about. I was getting really attached to the idea of staying in one place long enough to form traditions. It occurred to me that going to college had always been about escaping Mom, and now I was finally in a place I didn't want to leave. There was only one year of high school left and for the first time in my life, I was suddenly unsure what I wanted to do after graduation. I was only really sure of one thing: No matter where I went or what I chose, I wanted Maura to be part of the decision.

With all the dock spots taken up by weekend campers and Maura and I free of any gear, Luke pulled the boat as far into the shallow as he could without letting the motor hit bottom.

"You'll have to hop in the water and walk to shore. Wish I could take you via the dock but it doesn't look like anyone's willing to jeopardize their spot on a day this nice."

"Not a problem," said Maura, leaning down to untie her hikers. With our shoes and socks in one hand and a small pack of essentials in the other, Maura and I hopped off the back of the boat and into the waist-deep water.

"How will you get back across?" asked Luke.

Maura motioned to the Ranger card in the pocket of her light blue flannel shirt. "We'll call the station for a ride when we're finished."

"Text me when you get off Cascade Highway and are headed toward Bend," said Nick, and gave us his cell number.

"Let us know if you find your Dad, okay?" said Luke. "Give us a happy ending to close out the weekend."

"Sure," said Maura, a sad smile making its way across her face. It was a promise she couldn't make and yet one she wasn't ready not to make either. With a kiss on the cheek for each of them from Maura and a wave goodbye from me, we gave Jagged Little Pill one last shove from shore. We watched as it drifted out past the playing children, Toby Keith blaring from the speaker towers. Luke and the boys hit the accelerator and the bow of the boat rose over the water, its giant wake making waves for the giggling toddlers wading at the shoreline. Soon it was just Maura and I standing waist deep in sun warmed water, ready at last to face what lay ahead.

Chapter Thirty-eight: Maura

As soon as we turned our back on the water and began wading toward the beach, it was abundantly clear that we weren't going to find my father near the waterline. Cultus Lake may have been a dot on the map twenty years ago, but it wasn't a secret anymore. Just as Luke had warned, the beach was packed with weekenders. Every camp spot was full, every dock bumper to bumper with boats. There were even boats anchored between the docks where campers had arrived too late to secure an actual dock spot, but were still willing to throw out an anchor and mark their territory. I could see why they wanted to stay here so badly. The lake, though big and busy, was a beauty. When you stood on the shore, looking out across the water there were no signs of city life. You couldn't even see the Lodge across the way from here, just the never-ending water, trees, and the uninterrupted blue of the sky.

The whole place was pulsating with the sounds of children laughing, splashing, and screaming along the shore. Out on the water, boats tore through the surf, their stereo systems echoing as they swung past the campgrounds, making their way to the ski course that lined the right hand curve of the lake. Wherever my father was, it was quieter, isolated, peaceful. He'd have appreciated the culture of all these families enjoying a break from the rest of society, but he wouldn't have wanted to camp among them. I knew him too well to think that.

That didn't mean the people couldn't be of use. If Luke was correct and at least a handful of campers were truly regulars, there was a chance they would have some insight as to where to find Dad, and if we were really lucky someone would remember him. With Alex beside me, we headed into camp. There were no roads here, just well-travelled dirt paths connecting one campsite to another. The lucky campers had spots by the lake with fire pits, easy outhouse access and picnic tables to dine on. The not so lucky campers were stationed in the trees, their tents tilting awkwardly over roots and other particles of forest not intended for sleeping on. It was these particular campers who caught my eye. From the center of the tree line camp, a tall balding man in tiny running shorts and an Estacada track T-shirt pulled a long shiny whistle from his neckline. With three harsh toots, he called the campers forth from their tents. All around us teens popped out of igloos, each attired in clothing fit for a track meet not vacation. The man with the whistle clapped his hands together to gain the attention of the campers.

"Circle up!" he yelled. "Junior Varsity, you'll be taking the lake trail this morning with Captain Alexis. Watch-out for roots along the way. Not all of these trails are well maintained. There isn't much point in coming out here to train if you're gonna sprain your ankle before the season even starts. Varsity, you'll be headed up Cultus Mountain which Coach Grady." Groaning erupted all around. "Hey!" he yelled. "If you've got something better to do I'm sure our JV runners would be willing to swap you places this fall." As quickly as the groaning began it came to a halt. "Grab water, hit the outhouse, whatever you need. We'll be moving out in five minutes, not a second later." All around the coach teens scattered, some to lace up, while others made a beeline for the bathroom.

I was well- in cross country training regimens. These kids weren't here for vacation (although a cross country trip like this would have been pretty bad ass), they were here to try out new terrain before the season started, and that meant there was a good chance they had been all over this lake. Ever afraid that any adult worth their salt would call the authorities rather than help Alex and I find Dad, I opted to bypass the coach and see what I could find out from the kids. On a stump to my right, the student Captain the coach had referenced in his directions was busy lacing up a pair of well-worn ASICS running shoes.

"Alexis, right?" Alexis straightened up at the sound of her name. She had to be a senior to have gained captain status. Alexis wore her long blond hair tied back in a ponytail, wispy bangs held back by a hot pink Nike sweatband. She was the perfect shape for a runner: Thin but not too thin, muscular but not bulky, flat as a board, which was a curse for dating but a blessing when it came to competition. If I had Alexis's body maybe I'd have placed better in last year's regionals. As it was, I took third in my division - not too shabby for a girl whose training could be described as minimal.

"Have we met?" asked Alexa, clearly confused.

"No. Sorry, I'm Maura and this is Alex," I gestured toward Alex beside me. "We're looking for someone and we thought if you've been hitting the trails around here you might have seen him."

"I don't pay all that much attention to my surroundings when I'm running. We pretty much focus on the out and back."

"I understand, but if I described him, would you just listen and see if it rings any bells?"

Alexis let out a heavy breath. "Sure, just make it quick. We've got to head out in a minute."

I did my best to describe Dad and what his camp might potentially look like as quickly as possible.

Alexis shrugged. "Sorry. There's a good chance he's out there, but I don't remember seeing him. Someone else might have," she offered. "You can try asking around." With that Alexis was off to round up the rest of Junior Varsity.

"Do you want to ask anyone else?" said Alex, but it was already too late. All around us kids were lining up to head out. To our right, the Varsity crew wasted no time following Coach Grady in a steady ascent out of camp and up the mountain. To our left, JV diligently followed Alexis as she wound past the outhouse and toward the lake trail. I started to tell Alex we might as well follow in the same direction as Alexis when I felt a tap on my shoulder. I turned to find a spindly kid in running shorts, no shirt and a red bandanna.

"Yes?" I inquired.

"I didn't mean to eavesdrop but I think I can help you."

"Seriously?!" I asked.

"Maybe," he responded. "Are you looking for a guy with a limp?"

"Yes!" said Alex and I in tandem.

"Well, I don't know if he's still there, but I saw him about a week ago. He's camped at Deer Lake. It's not that far from here. We ran there the first week we were here. I biffed it majorly hopping over a log. He patched me up and showed me which trail to take to get back to camp. Nice guy. That's your Dad?"

"I hope so," I said.

"Well," said the boy. "I have to go before they get too far for me to catch up to. The trail to Deer Lake is up that way," he said, pointing past the lakeside campgrounds. "Just follow the path till you run out of campsites and there will be a sign. The whole hike won't take you more than half an hour."

The second the boy was out of my sight; I was ready to sprint the two miles to Deer Lake. Alex, however, was not so inclined.

"Maura!" he said urgently, grabbing me by the wrist. "I know you want to find your Dad, but I can't keep up with you for two miles in those mosquito-infested woods. Can we please just walk this one?"

As much as I wanted to break free of his grip and tell him "meet you at the top," I knew that sprinting wasn't going to change what we found when we got there. Alex had been darn near perfect coming on this trip, chasing me from lake to lake, hopping on strangers' bikes, dealing with my attitude when I snapped for no reason. I couldn't very well tell him to go shove it now when we were this close.

"We can walk," I said, taking his hand in my own.

Chapter Thirty-nine: Alex

Hand in hand, we made the final ascent toward Maura's father. The fact that the boy from the cross country team had not only seen Mike recently but interacted with him gave the two of us a sort of hope I hadn't dared to consider until this moment. The truth was that no matter how many times I said we were looking for Maura's father, somewhere in the back of my brain I had already acknowledged that what we were looking for was his remains.

Now, we were looking for the man, his campsite, and one hell of an explanation as to how he could have left his kids, father and brother alone with only their worst fears to keep them company.

We hiked in silence over the troll bridge, deep into the woods, past the last straggling tents of hermit campers willing to brave the bugs to avoid the people. Every half mile or so we came across another sign for Deer Lake. With each sign I became more and more aware that we were that much closer to the end of our journey. Was it terrible to admit that I didn't want it to end? I wanted to spend the next six months traveling the wilderness with Maura. Curling up next to her these past two nights had been the best sleep I'd had in a long time. I knew that we wouldn't end just because this trip did, that when we returned to Pendleton we would still see each other, and likely we would grow closer. But I also knew that there would never be a time like this again. We'd had 72 hours most kids only dream about. We'd made friends, challenged ourselves, learned what made the other one tick. We had danced on a lake in the moonlight, for Christ's sake. The rest of the world seemed small and insignificant compared to these last 72 hours. I wanted to drag my feet but that wasn't fair to Maura. What had been a grand romantic adventure for me was surely wrought with fear, frustration and heartache for her. My job now was to help her face whatever lay ahead, whether it be a blowout with her father or an onslaught of tears.

Try as I may to avoid it, each step brought us closer to our final destination. Deer Lake was three hundred feet ahead, but we didn't need to reach the sign to know we had arrived. There, in the clearing behind a small picnic table and fire pit, stood a tent for one. Its bright orange fabric was unmistakable among the green of the trees. I gave Maura's hand a squeeze as we trekked the final distance.

Mike wasn't in camp when we got there. Aside from the sounds of birds flitting through the trees and critters skittering across the pines, the camp remained eerily silent. Unlike everywhere else we had been in the Cascade Lakes, there was no steady sound of gentle waves lapping against the shore. Deer Lake, after all, didn't have a boat ramp or docks. If you wanted a boat here you had to pack it up from Cultus Lake, and it certainly wasn't big enough for anything with an engine. The lake was so small that with the right ambition you could swim directly across it.

Anxious to find signs of life, Maura began to evaluate the camp. Mike's bike wasn't anywhere nearby which meant he was likely out for the day hunting, or possibly fishing off one of the rocks on the far side. From the looks of his food supply, Mike would have had to hunt to eat at this point. The plastic tub Maura had packed him his last day home was down to two cans of pork and beans, half a bag of rice and a massive half eaten container of pistachios, the shells of which could be found littering the fire pit.

Beside the fire Mike, had cut himself a stump for a chair. The axe he'd used was still wedged in a nearby log. I sat down for a moment, trying to put myself in Mike's shoes, imagining what he must have imagined, sitting out here alone for all that time. It was during this contemplation that I first noticed a bizarre handmade structure sitting just to the right of Mike's stump chair.

"Hey Maura?" I called. "There's something here I think you oughta see." Maura popped out from the orange tent where she'd gone looking for further evidence of her father's whereabouts. As she came closer, I pointed to the small wooden lean-to. "What do you suppose that's for?"

Maura laughed. "I have no idea. Oh my God," cried Maura upon closer inspection. "Is that a tiny table? Did my Dad whittle a tiny shed and table? What the hell?" Maura burst out laughing, real guttural laughter, the kind of laughter I rarely got to hear from her. "I think he's lost his damn mind out here!"

"Is that stale bread?" I asked

"Bread?"

"On the tiny table."

Maura picked up the tiny white chunk sitting in the center of the whittled table. With an incredulous expression she inspected the crusty lump between her thumb and forefinger. "I guess...I guess so."

"Your dad is either feeding something very small or building a replica of the last supper."

Maura was a fit of giggles. "I don't know which is worse."

Maura came up empty handed in the tent. Aside from Mike's medication, which he stored in the mesh sack that hung above his sleeping bag, there were very few identifiable possessions. If he had brought his wallet out here with him, he kept it on him at all times and, to the best of Maura's knowledge, he had refused to bring his cell phone with him on the trip. He was smart like that. Had he brought his phone we could have reported him missing and tracked his location anytime he turned his phone on. The fact that he didn't bring a phone made it abundantly clear that he did not wish to be found. If something had happened to Mike out here, those prescriptions would have been the only way of discerning him from any other John Doe gone missing in the forest.

The longer we sat around camp the more restless Maura grew. The way I saw it, there was no sense in looking for Mike.

We'd located his camp and it would be getting dark in a few hours. We couldn't miss him, not when he would have to return to make supper, go to bed, and possibly visit with his imaginary friends (that part worried me a little). With that in mind, I suggested Maura and I go for a swim.

"You want to go swimming?" she asked.

"Yeah, why not. It's like, 90 degrees out here, we've been hiking for three days and aside from hopping out of Luke's boat we haven't so much as taken a dip."

"Alex, we have to wait for my dad."

I suspected it would be difficult to talk Maura into leaving, now that we were so close to seeing Mike, but the way I saw it, the more relaxed she was when his bike spun into camp the better.

"Look, if your dad gets back to camp before we do, that won't change anything. Besides, if he doesn't get back till much later, you'll be grateful we burnt some time. We'll go stir crazy just sitting here waiting."

Maura mulled it over. "And we'll come right back after?"

"Of course."

"Okay, we swim. But just for a little while."

"Understood."

Mike's camp was close enough to the water that we could swim without really leaving camp at all, but the ground was muddy and the water murky in the alcove of trees that surrounded Mike's site. I lifted my hand to shield my eyes from the sun and better my view of the other side. There were tall rocks suitable for climbing about a half mile to our right. They would have made a great fishing spot for Mike. They were going to make an even better diving point for Maura and me.

"Come along you. Our swimming hole awaits."

Maura rolled her eyes. "You know neither of us have our stuff. I'm not wearing a swimsuit nor am I planning to engage in any skinny dipping. Just imagine my father comes around the corner and there I am, skinny dipping in the middle of nowhere - with a boy! - when I'm supposed to be at home watching Natalie."

"A, your dad doesn't get to judge your makeshift parenting choices on account of they are totally and completely his responsibilities, not yours and B, God has given us underwear to swim in. Plus, you can wear your tank top in the water and borrow something from your dad's bag when we get back."

"You want me to swim in my underwear?"

"It isn't any worse than a swimsuit. Besides, I promise not to stare too long at anything I'm not supposed to be looking at."

"Wow...that's really reassuring," she replied, sarcasm dripping from every word.

"No more stalling. Time for fun."

Together we followed the short bike trail to the diving rocks. The water was deeper on this side, the rocks jutting out just far enough to make jumping a possibility. It would be a scramble to the top, but I'd seen Maura drive a boat, ride a dirt bike, and start a campfire without fear. My guess was the girl wasn't afraid of a little harness-free climbing.

"You climb up first. I'll change down here and come up behind you. And Alex, I swear to God, if you peek I'll send you back to meet my dad minus the family jewels."

"You're very charming when you're being terrifying," I replied, taking her chin between my hands and popping a kiss on her forehead. "Rest easy. I won't peek at your delicates." With that I began my climb up the rock. It wasn't more than 12 feet up, but there weren't a lot of great footholds. It took me nearly five minutes to get to the top. Five minutes of Maura watching my every move with great interest. Once I had reached the top, I did as told and faced away from Maura and out toward the lake while she changed and readied herself to climb.

Deer Lake wasn't as charming as the others we had been to. Maybe it was the fact that we were looking at it in the daylight, void of the stars and moon that had made the last two nights so special, but I didn't find the lake as magical as Mike had. It must have been different all those years ago, when he came here with his then fully-intact family. Maybe it was the company that made it special for him and not the place itself. I wondered if he thought about that once he got out here. Had he been disappointed? Had he really thought it would be like it was then? You can never go back. All the great movies, books, and songs tell you that much.

Down below I could hear the rustle of clothing being removed. In conjunction, I peeled off my own Red Rocks T-shirt, folding it nicely and piling it beneath my cargo shorts. I sat on the edge of the rock, my feet dangling off the edge, to wait for Maura. The sun felt glorious on my face and beneath my bare legs as I warmed myself on the sunbaked rocks. I was in the process of reclining back onto my elbows when I first felt a dry, crumbly substance beneath my palm. I sat upright to inspect, not wanting to be elbow deep in animal excrement or whatever else had managed to root itself on this rock. There shouldn't have been any mud on the rocks. I knew that because no plant life could sustain itself this exposed to the sun, this high from the water. I wanted it to be mud but the longer I looked, the longer I was sure that the thick, dark substance adhering itself to my palm came from a man and not the earth. I felt my stomach turn as I stood to look for what I knew I would find, but couldn't bear the thought of. With my heart in my throat I peered over the edge, not across the water like before, not toward the sky where birds flitted in the warm afternoon air. No, this time I looked down to the base of the rock where Maura's father lay mangled in the overgrowth.

Chapter Forty: Maura

From the top of the rock Alex screamed down at me. "Stay where you are Maura!"

I tried to scramble up, worried that something had happened, worried that Alex was hurt. But he was down the rock before I could so much as get my foot in the first hold. Then he jumped. He jumped from 12 feet to stop me from climbing, and it was. then I knew Alex wasn't the one in trouble. It was then that I noticed my father's bike propped against the tree to our right. Then that I read the desperation in Alex's wild and worried eyes. Then that I knew my father was dead and I was too late to save him.

Chapter Forty-one: Alex

We didn't talk on the way back to Mike's camp. I have nothing to say and Maura is nonfunctional. A walking, breathing robot, dead behind the eyes. She didn't ask to see the body and I'm glad because I wouldn't want her to see her father like that. I'll never unsee Mike at the bottom of that ravine, his right leg twisted in a grotesque position, dried blood caked in his hair, his fishing pole still caught in the lake grass, unable to drift out, the same way his body was unable to drift out.

How long had he been there? Baking in the sun? Lying in the weeds? He had slipped, broken his ankle for sure, but did the impact to the head kill him or had he suffered, unable to move, unable to return to camp? We didn't get to know those things. It wasn't a movie. There wouldn't be a man in a white lab jacket explaining the details of his death so we could all understand. He slipped. He fell. He died. Two girls would live without a father now.

There were things to be done. People to call. Not for Maura, though. Maura could do nothing, but I could do that much. Once we arrived back at Mike's camp, she changed from her blue flannel to her father's camo hunting jacket, crawled into his sleeping bag and cried herself to sleep. I waited till her breathing grew heavy before leaving her and heading back down to Big Cultus where our cell signal was strongest.

From the dock in front of the Cross Country Team's camp site, I first called Grandpa. There was no calling Child Protective Services now. He promised to take good care of Natalie and encouraged me to let Maura take her time. After Grandpa, I used the card the ranger had given us earlier to let the forestry department know what had happened, where to recover the body and who to contact when it was ready to be picked up in Bend. It was Ranger Armstrong who answered. He offered to pick us up at the dock in a few hours when we were ready.

It was early afternoon when I returned to Mike's camp. Maura had managed to drag herself out of the tent, though she still wore her father's jacket. In her hand she held a well-worn leather journal. I pulled a log over to the fire to sit beside her.

"Is that your Dad's?"

"Mm-hmm," she said. There were still tears coursing down her cheeks but at least the all-out convulsing from earlier had ceased.

"Did you read it?"

"Most of it. Some of it I couldn't. He didn't plan to come back, Alex, but I don't think he meant to die that way either."

"No, no, I don't think so either. It was an accident, Maura." Gently I wrapped my arm around her shoulder. I wanted to pull her in close, hold her till it stopped hurting, but we both knew that wasn't possible.

She jerked from my grasp. "But he didn't plan to come back!" she yelled, slamming the journal on the ground beside her. "He wrote it all down. He never planned to come back, "she said, her voice filling with a cold tone I'd not heard before.

"He loved you Maura."

"Not enough."

Chapter Forty-two: Maura

Maybe when the anger stopped I wouldn't hate him. But then what? Grief? Was grief any better? Would his mother be proud that he'd left his children to come out here and die with her memory? I never knew my grandmother. Dad hadn't been much younger than me when she died. How could he forget what it felt like? Didn't he realize the grief that ate him alive would become Natalie and mine once he was gone?

This and a million other thoughts went through my head as we packed up Dad's camp. I carefully packed the journal in my supply bag, unwilling to let it out of my sight. I looked over at Alex, who was wrapping the squirrel home in my father's pillowcase for safe keeping.

"What are you going to do with that?" I asked.

"Something for Natalie," he said, a small smile playing across his face. "It's the last thing he made. I thought she might like it."

I smiled despite myself. It would give her a little peace. I knew that, so why had it been Alex who thought of it and not me? I had been a mother to Natalie for as long as I could remember, but I didn't think I was ready to be both parents, not at seventeen, not with our father's death hanging over us like a dark cloud always on the cusp of torrential downpour.

"It wasn't the last thing," I said.

"What do you mean?" asked Alex.

"In the journal. There was one last entry. Dated three days ago. I didn't read it. I couldn't read it. Not after the one before. Not after he made it abundantly clear that he would rather die alone out here than stay till the end with us."

"You'll read it when you're ready, Maura."

"Yeah well, it's time to go now."

With only what we could carry on our backs, we took one last look at Dad's final campsite. I pictured him by the fire each morning, whittling that tiny table. I pictured him standing from the rock, casting his line into the water each morning, that satisfied expression he got on his face whenever he felt the first bite on the other end of the line. I pictured him bandaging the cross country kid's knee - always the caregiver, always the compassionate one - and lastly, I pictured him as a child, the way he was in that photo by the lake, his mother beside him, the two of them eternally watching waves lap the shore while the rest of the world slept.

Chapter Forty-three: Alex

With Maura following behind in Mike's truck, we rolled down Cascade Highway for the final time. I watched Maura in the rearview mirror. She never once looked back, not when we passed Lava Lake, not when we passed Green Lake, not even when three familiar dirt bikes pulled up beside us, honking and wailing as Nick, Aiden, and Tom shouted goodbye and good riddance in a cloud of dust and gravel.

We didn't stop in Bend as we had originally planned. Instead we drove until I had to hit a rest stop or risk bursting. It was best, I figured, that the two of us took separate vehicles. I didn't have a father to lose but if I did, I imagined a few hours of solitary confinement might help sort the anger from the grief. I thought about George and our promise to stop at Shaniko Days on our way through. We wouldn't stop now.

Everything had changed in the last 72 hours. We were no longer on a search for her father, no longer filled with that mix of apprehension and excitement that drove us into the wilderness in the first place. But most of all, we were a we now. Somewhere along the way, Grandpa James, Maura, Natalie, and I had become a makeshift family. It was the first real family I'd ever had, and I planned to keep us together even if I didn't know what that entailed yet.

Chapter Forty-four: Maura

We hit Shaniko around 4 pm. The ghost town had come to life for Shaniko Days, just like George had said it would. Everywhere you looked the streets were lined with tents, campers, and people. Where they came from was anybody's guess. There were food vendors selling greasy curly fries in the shape of a brick, snow cones dripping in the August sun. The smell of barbecued chicken wafted through my open driver's side window, tempting me to pull aside just for a moment, just to feel normal. But today I didn't get to be normal.

I looked for George as we rolled past the museum, but he was nowhere to be found. It was his weekend after all, his once a year to show people the town he'd grown to love with every fiber of his being. I smiled at the thought of him walking people through the old car museum, spouting his favorite details about wool, making dozens of sandwiches for people who cared, and then I felt guilty for smiling when my father couldn't. As if he could read my mind, Alex gradually accelerated, leaving Shaniko in the rearview mirror as we continued on our path back to Pendleton, where Natalie waited for two people she cared about to return. How could I tell her it was just me now? Feeling the tears threatening to take over, I plugged my iPhone into Dad's auxiliary port and blasted Tom Petty as loud as the speakers would go. I knew all of Dad's favorite songs by heart. How many drives out to Grandpa Mick's had we taken with "American Girl" blasting from the speakers, my father singing along in his best/worst falsetto? Why couldn't I remember the last drive or the last song? Why couldn't I remember the last fucking moment that mattered? As much as I wanted to avoid it, I was keenly aware that my father was slowly fading from a person to a memory.

It was the end of August and Pendleton was busy shifting from summer to fall, the first signs of next month's big rodeo beginning to line our streets. Soon we would have our own version of Shaniko Days, as people from near and far came streaming into town for the Pendleton Round-Up. For now, however, it was still quiet, still small. As we drove down Main Street, I caught sight of Elizabeth and Nikka sipping smoothies outside of the Great Pacific. I honked at her from the stop light. With her thumb and pinkie she made the call me sign and I would. I would call her this time because I was beginning to get the feeling that friendship was about to become more important to me now that my family had shrunk by one.

I parked Dad's truck out back and met Alex in Mr. James' driveway. Hand in hand we made our way up the porch steps. The door was open despite the bugs that swarmed the riverside this time of year. I recognized Sesame Street playing on the TV long before we entered the living room to catch Big Bird prancing down the street greeting puppets and people along the way. There on the couch with half-eaten salisbury steak TV dinners in front of them lay Natalie and Grandpa James.

Grandpa James sawing logs while Natalie dozed slumped against his side, her arms wrapped tight around a plush version of Twilight Sparkle, her favorite My Little Pony. It was new and likely the reason for the quaint smile that stretched across her face, even in sleep.

With my free hand I made the shush signal to Alex and led him through to the back porch. There was no sense in waking them now. Let her have one last sleep before we rattled her world.

We took a seat on the back porch steps, watching in silence as the sun set over the Umatilla River below us. My life was forever changed for the worse, but for one blissful moment I was aware that beside me sat the loveliest of silver linings.

"I'm glad you're staying Alex." I told him, turning to look him in the eye for the first time since we'd found my father's body. Without words and without hesitation he took my face into his hands and pressed his lips to mine. Our first kiss, soft, gentle, and full of mourning gave me the courage to read the final entry in my father's journal.

Chapter Forty-five: Mike's Journal

Last night I dreamt of my daughters. I dreamt of their futures, their families, their successes. I dreamt of the mighty young women they would become and the mighty young women they already were. In my dreams, my children had grown like blackberry bushes, resilient and determined despite me, despite my failures. They took what little bit of water I gave them and they used it to thrive. They didn't need me to be successful, they didn't even need me to survive. They were after all, an invasive species. But that didn't mean they didn't deserve care. Just because I knew for certain that they *could* do it alone didn't mean I had to let them.

Last night when I dreamt of my daughters I dreamt of their futures and they included me.

About the Author

M.F. Lorson lives and works as a Youth Services Librarian in the Pacific Northwest. The Hunter's Daughter is her second Young Adult novel. To check out Lorson's other work please visit www.mflorson.weebly.com. Special thanks to Ellen Mosier who edited this title and Sarah Woodbury for both formatting *The Hunter's Daughter* and serving as a mentor.

Made in the USA
San Bernardino, CA
14 February 2018